Fair Play

A NOVEL

Tove Jansson

Sort Of
BOOKS

Fair Play

A NOVEL

Tove Jansson

Translated from the Swedish by
Thomas Teal

Introduced by
Ali Smith

Thanks

Ali Smith thanks: my friend Kathleen Bryson who, several years ago, looked at me in wide eyed amazement when I said I'd never read anything by Tove Jansson, immediately took me downstairs to the children's department in a bookshop on Charing Cross Road, bought me *Moominsummer Madness*, told me about *The Summer Book* (which had been out of print for decades and proved very hard to find) and also about "a beautiful novel Jansson wrote about two women artists who live and work together", which she'd read in its original Swedish some years before.

Sort of Books thanks: Sophia Jansson, Helen Svensson of Schildts, Ali Smith, Kathleen Bryson and Thomas Teal; Peter Dyer, Henry Iles, Miranda Davies and Tim Chester for production; and Holly Marriott and Jason Craig at Penguin.

FILI (Finnish Literature Information Centre) has supported the translation of this book.

Photo credits

Inside front cover: Tove Jansson and Tuulikki Pietilä © Per Olov Jansson
Inside back cover: Seascape © Margareta Strömstedt; Tove Jansson potting © Beata Bergström; other four photos of Tove Jansson © Per Olov Jansson; flowers on Klovharu © Pentti Eistola.
p.1 (cat) © Tuulikki Pietilä
p.17 (Tove Jansson in Italy, 1979) © Pentti Eistola
p.128 (shore) © Tuulikki Pietilä

This English translatinon first published in 2007 by
Sort Of Books, PO Box 18678, London NW3 2FL.

Distributed by the Penguin Group in all territories excluding the US and Canada: Penguin Books, 80 Strand, London WC2R 0RL.

Typeset in Goudy and GillSans to a design by Henry Iles.
Printed in Italy by Legoprint.

128pp
A catalogue record for this book is available from the British Library
ISBN 978-0-95489-953-0

"*Fair Play* could in fact be called a novel of friendship, of rather happy tales about two women who share a life of work, delight and consternation. They are very unlike each other, but perhaps that is why they manage to play the game successfully, with patience and, of course, a great deal of love."

Original cover copy by Tove Jansson

Contents

Introduction

by Ali Smith

Labora et amare. Work and love: the motto Tove Jansson
worked into her own personal bookplate design in the 1940s
when she was starting out, a young artist. Fifty years later,
internationally famous as one of the world's most enduringly
imaginative and inspiring writers and illustrators, she still felt
much the same. As she told an interviewer in 1994, "the most
important thing for me has been work. And then love."

The publication of *Fair Play* in its first ever English
translation is a notable event and really cause for a
celebration. It's the first of Jansson's novels for adults to be
translated into English for over thirty years. Jansson published
Rent Spel (its original Swedish title) in 1989, when she was
herself in her mid-seventies (she died in 2001, aged 86). It
was the ninth of her eleven books written specifically for
adults, of which, until now, only three have reached full English
publication, most celebratedly her rich minimalist masterpiece
The Summer Book (1972) — a story, in typical Jansson mould,
about nothing much and yet about everything — about a child
and an old woman who spend a long, light summer together
on a tiny island off the coast of Finland.

Tove Jansson's artwork for the original
publication of **Rent spel** (*Fair Play*), 1989

Jansson has always been rightly feted for being the
brilliant children's author she is. Her tales of the Finn Family
Moomintroll and their extended alternative family, which
cared for everyone and everything from a tiny anarchist to a
hulking great Scandinavian melancholic monster, and survived
by inventiveness all sorts of catastrophes and existentialities,
made her justly internationally famous. But it is only now that
we're getting the chance to see how very fine her fiction
for adults is, too. It shares the clarity, the beneficence, the
imagination and the survivalist calm that made her writing for
children unique. It also displays her particular versatility, which
means a text by Jansson, whether meant for children or adults,
can be read with great pleasure and satisfaction by pretty
much anybody of any age.

But in her writing for adults Jansson was also, in her own
quiet way, quite radical both with form and subject matter.
Her preferred shape is an open form, in a language so tightly
edited that its clarity makes for mysterious transparency. Her
epics are almost transgressively, certainly anarchically, small and
unexpected, and her books deal on the whole with people
not usually included or given that much space in what we
might call the extended family of literature.

On the backs of the Penguin Puffin copies of the Moomin
tales, Jansson's biography used to say she lived and worked
alone on an island; actually she lived, both on her island
and in Helsinki, alongside her lifelong partner and travelling
companion, the graphic artist, Tuulikki Pietilä. The women spent
over 40 years together, working and travelling. "We always
took our sketch books with us wherever we went," Pietilä
wrote later, in a beautiful piece called "Travels with Tove",
where she remembers, among other things, how on one trip
Jansson jumped, full of typical enthusiasm, into the Atlantic
in January for a bathe (and contracted her usual bronchitis

afterwards), how they liked to avoid stuffy first class and would always sneak off to second class, where things were much more fun, how they shared a lot of unlikely adventures, once ending up bunking in a kind of youth hostel in Edinburgh even though they were quite old ladies by then – "but we looked young", as she says – and how they always made sure, wherever they were in the world, that they had enough money for cigarettes, and film for Pietilä's Konica camera. "Tove was always my best subject."

So what can happen when Tove Jansson turns her attention to her own favourite subjects, love and work, in the form of this novel about two women, lifelong partners and friends? Expect something philosophically calm – and something discreetly radical. At first sight it looks autobiographical. Like everything Jansson wrote, it's much more than it seems.

Is it a novel? Is it stories? It's both; it breaks the boundaries of both forms, in a series of linked vignettes about two women who live and work side by side in an equilibrium that's at once slight and revolutionary. "They lived at opposite ends of a large apartment building." Mari is a writer and illustrator. Jonna is a filmmaker and artist. Once again, not that much seems to happen. Mari and Jonna work a lot, watch films together, make films together, spend time on an island, travel the world, relive their youth, argue about their parents, go sailing, get caught in fog. Their stories dovetail and intertwine. They know each other's sleeping habits. They know each other's living and working habits. They honour these habits. They know that things are often uncontrollable, out of their hands, even on the tiniest island. They fight. They get a bit jealous. Things and people come between them. When this happens, they sort it out. The aesthetic and creative urge compels them, always. They put off work. They get irascible. They refuse each other and irritate each other, and are kind and tough with each other, so that both love and work are revealed as made of the little refusals and agreements that happen mundanely in the course of a shared life.

A lot isn't said. "Don't tell me things I already know," one says to the other, amiably. There's a lot that doesn't need to be said out loud. It's a novel with a profound sense of discretion at its core. But the flip side of silence is voice, and the flip side of nothing much happening, as always with Jansson, is that absolutely everything is happening. Take the first page of the first, typically unassuming story, "Changing Pictures", where Jonna rearranges the art on one of the walls of Mari's apartment. This novel is about creativity from the very start – about how you take a day, the same as all the other old one-after-the-other days, and make it really new and fresh, no matter what age you are, what life you're in. It features an immediate challenge to vision – it is very much about how to shake off old ways of seeing, how to see things differently, get rid of what's "hopelessly conventional" and replace it with something more hopeful. It is also a story full of the unselfish admiration of another, from the word go. Jonna is blithely uncompromising (as Mari will be, in other chapters), and in her art, or in her editing of Mari's living space, she makes something come alive with "a completely new significance ... almost provocative".

The book opens, then, on a simple little story about letting someone change things, which becomes a story about the editing process, or about how to make art – and is for the length of the book a parable about how to renew mundane life. Its inference is also emotional. "Look, here's a thing of mine and here's your drawing, and they clash. We need distance; it's essential." *Fair Play* is often an excellent handbook of advice and rules for the workings of art – but it's never just about aesthetic wisdom. It's also very much about emotional wisdom.

So many of its vignettes are about how to bring art and life together into a working relationship. And so much of it is about these concepts held in its new title, fairness and playfulness. The "blend of perfectionism and nonchalance" that Mari sees in Jonna is apparent all through Jansson's own writing style – perfectly caught itself by Thomas Teal, a luminous translator of Jansson's twin talent for surface and depth, simplicity and reverberation in language, and someone who knows exactly how to convey her gift for sensing the meaning embedded in the most mundane act or turn of phrase.

"Fog", for instance, is literally a chapter about being lost in fog, and lost, too, to the fog of an old, old argument. It becomes a story about what's not sayable, a story that admits some things are veiled, fogged, not resolvable. *Fair Play* allows for life's unresolvables at the same time as being very much about aesthetic resolution and composition. The chapters are thoughtfully, deceptively casually, arranged to arise as if by accident out of each other. They seem like throwaway pieces of time. Of course, this is one of *Fair Play*'s themes – the recording of haphazard life and what it means, at all, to record anything. The cumulative effect is to suggest that there's always more life, more possibility, another story, and that nothing is fixed or ended. There's always something new to know or see, even when you think you've seen it all. The openness of this book's structure, when you reach its end, is both liberating and moving.

It's also a novel very much about "unexplored territory", something Jansson will have been very aware of in the writing of these stories about friendship between women, and something which so fascinates Jonna in her love of B-movie Westerns and their repeating of clichés about endless honourable "friendship between men". But the keys to this particular new territory are the opposite of cliché. Openness, playfulness and space are concepts which come up repeatedly through the novel. "Give these ladies some space!" yells a barmaid in Phoenix on one of the explorative adventures Mari and Jonna have. "They're from Finland." It's as if *Fair Play* knows it's a kind of foreign territory in itself. So many of these stories are about the giving of space to another person, the kind of space that only someone who loves properly and openly can give. "There are empty spaces that must be respected – those often long periods when a person can't see the pictures or find the words and needs to be left alone." There's also crucial space between Mari and the narrator, which is what gives this book its essential meditative nature.

But it is, too, a piece of writing about time running out, about the end of living space, about inevitable ends. The chapter called "Cemeteries", for instance, examines how we helplessly think we can order things and control our fates; *Fair Play* never ignores real bleakness. Part of its analysis of art knows that art makes a killing in the same way as a pin will through a butterfly. Part of its radicalism comes from the repeated admittance that its main characters are simply getting older. Yet the form of the book suggest there'll be no stopping. There's only the journey, the open travelling companionship, the long-running aesthetic argument and agreement between Jonna and Mari, "doing all right", from the start of the book to its finish.

Consider the gentleness of this work, the twinned humility and understatement in what it actually means to be "doing all right". Jansson deals with its relationship with care, humour and, above all, affectionate discretion. *Fair Play* is, in the end, a huge, yet astoundingly discreet, declaration of a good-working love, a homage to the kind of coupledom that rarely receives such homage, and at the same time a homage to the everyday weather, the light, the skies, the countless bad movies and good movies of living and working well with someone for the length of an adult life.

Labora et amare. "They sat opposite each other at the table without talking." Kindness passes between them unspoken. It's a relationship that works. Its final chapter, in which one, without so much as saying it, grants the other the necessary space to work – in other words, to be herself – reveals not just the size and truth of the love but the revolutionary freedom that comes with such love.

Fair Play is a very fine art.

Tove Jansson in Padua, Italy, 1979

Fair Play

A NOVEL

Tove Jansson

Translated from the Swedish by
Thomas Teal

Changing pictures

JONNA HAD A HAPPY HABIT OF WAKING EACH MORNING as if to a new life. which stretched before her straight through to evening, clean, untouched, rarely shadowed by yesterday's worries and mistakes.

Another habit – or rather a gift, equally surprising – was her flood of unexpected and completely spontaneous ideas. Each lived and blossomed powerfully for a time until suddenly swept aside by a new impulse demanding its own undeniable space. Like now this business about the frames. Several months earlier, Jonna had decided she wanted to frame some of the pictures by fellow artists that Mari had on her walls. She made some very pretty frames, but when they were ready to hang, Jonna was seized by new ideas and the pictures were left standing around on the floor.

"For the time being," Jonna said. "And for that matter, your whole collection needs rehanging, top to bottom. It's hopelessly conventional." Mari waited and said nothing. In fact, it felt good having things unfinished, a little as if she had just moved in and didn't have to take the thing so seriously.

And over the years, she'd learned not to interfere with Jonna's plans and their mysterious blend of perfectionism and nonchalance, a mix not everyone can properly appreciate. Some people just shouldn't be disturbed in their inclinations, whether large or small. A reminder can instantly turn enthusiasm into aversion and spoil everything.

Pursuing her work in blessed seclusion, free from interference; moulding and playing with all sorts of materials, a game that all at once, capriciously, could become irresistible and crowd out all other activity. Enjoying a sudden burst of practical energy and repairing everything broken in the house and in the apartments of her completely impractical friends – mending things or making them beautiful, or simply, to everyone's relief, discarding them. Periods of nothing but intense reading, night and day. Periods of listening to music to the exclusion of all else. To name just a few.

And each and every one of these periods was sharply defined by a day or two of extreme unease and boredom, irresolute days in search of a new course. It was always the same; there was no other way. To encroach on those empty days with suggestions or advice was utterly unthinkable.

Once Mari happened to observe, "You do only what you like."

"Naturally," Jonna said, "of course I do." And she smiled at Mari in mild astonishment.

And now came the day in November when everything in Mari's studio was to be rehung, rearranged, renewed, and given a completely new significance – graphics, paintings, photographs, children's drawings, and all sorts of precious small objects reverently pinned up on the walls, which as time passed had lost all memory and meaning. Mari had assembled hammer, nails, picture hooks, steel wire, a level, and several other tools. Jonna had brought only a tape measure.

She said, "We'll start with the wall of honour. Naturally, that will stay strictly symmetrical. But your grandfather and grandmother are too far apart, and for that matter it can rain in on your grandfather through the stovepipe. And your mother's little wash drawing gets lost; it needs to be higher. That pretty mirror is idiotic, it doesn't belong, we have to keep it austere. The sword's okay, if a little pathetic. Here, measure – it'll be seven, or six and a half. Give me the awl."

Mari gave her the awl and saw how the wall regained a balance that was no longer traditional but instead almost provocative.

"Now," said Jonna. "Now we'll remove these little curiosities you don't really care about. Free up the walls. This will be an exhibition without a lot of knickknacks all over the place. Put them in one of your seashell boxes or send them to some children's museum."

Mari thought quickly about whether she should be offended or relieved, couldn't decide, and said nothing. Jonna moved on, took pictures down and put them back up, her hammer blows inaugurating a new era.

"I know," she said, "rejection's not easy. But you reject words, whole pages, long impossible stories, and it feels good once it's done. It's no different rejecting pictures, a picture's right to hang on a wall. And most of these have hung here too long; you don't even see them any more. The best stuff you have, you don't see any more. And they kill each other because they're badly hung. Look, here's a thing of mine and here's your drawing, and they clash. We need distance, it's essential. And different periods need distance to set them apart – unless you're just cramming them together for the shock effect! You simply have to feel it… There should be an element of surprise when people's eyes move across a wall covered with pictures. We don't want to make it too easy for them. Let them catch their breath and look again because they can't help it. Make them think, make them mad, even… Now we'll give our colleagues here better light. Why did you leave so much space right here?"

"I don't know," Mari said. But she did know. Suddenly she knew very well that deep down she didn't like the painter colleagues who had done these undeniably very fine works. Mari began paying attention. As she watched Jonna rehang the pictures, it seemed to her that lots of things, including their life together, fell into perspective and into place, a summary expressed in distance or self-evident clustering. The room had changed completely.

When Jonna had taken her tape home with her, Mari marvelled all evening at how easy it is in the end to understand the simplest things.

Videomania

THEY LIVED AT OPPOSITE ENDS OF A LARGE APARTMENT building near the harbour, and between their studios lay the attic, an impersonal no-man's-land of tall corridors with locked plank doors on either side. Mari liked wandering across the attic; it drew a necessary, neutral interval between their domains. She could pause on the way to listen to the rain on the metal roof, look out across the city as it lit its lights, or just linger for the pleasure of it.

They never asked, "Were you able to work today?" Maybe they had, twenty or thirty years earlier, but they'd gradually learned not to. There are empty spaces that must be respected – those often long periods when a person can't see the pictures or find the words and needs to be left alone.

When Mari came in, Jonna was on a ladder building shelves in her front hall. Mari knew that when Jonna started putting up shelves she was approaching a period of work. Of course the hall would be far too narrow and cramped, but that was immaterial. The last time, it was shelves in the bedroom and the result had been a series of excellent woodcuts. She glanced into the bathroom as she passed, but Jonna had not yet put printing paper in to soak, not yet. Before Jonna could do her graphic work in peace, she always spent some time printing up sets of earlier, neglected works – a job that had been set aside so she could focus on new ideas. After all, a period of creative grace can be short. Suddenly, and without warning, the pictures disappear, or they're chased away by some interference – someone or something that irretrievably cuts off the fragile desire to capture an observation, an insight.

Mari went back to the hall and said she had bought milk and paper towels, two steaks, and a nailbrush, and it was raining.

"Good," Jonna said. She hadn't heard. "Could you grab that other end for a second? Thanks. This is going to be a new shelf for videos. Nothing but videos. Did I mention Fassbinder's on tonight? What do you think? Should I build it right out to the door?"

"Yes, do. What time?"

"Nine-twenty."

About eight they remembered Alma's dinner. Jonna phoned her. "I'm sorry to call so late," she said, "but you know, Fassbinder's on this evening, and it's the last time... What? No, that won't work; we have to be here to cut out the commercials... Yes, it's really too bad. But you know how I loathe those commercials; they can ruin the whole film. Say hello to everyone. We'll see you... Yes, I will. Have fun. So long."

"Was she mad?" Mari asked.

"Oh, you know. Apparently the woman hasn't a clue about Fassbinder."

"Should we unplug the phone?"

"If you want. Nobody's going to call. They know better. Anyway, we don't have to answer."

The spring evenings had grown long, and it was hard to darken the room. They sat in their separate chairs and waited for Fassbinder, their silence a respectful preparation. They had waited this way for their meetings with Truffaut, Bergman, Visconti, Renoir, Wilder, and all the other honoured guests that Jonna had chosen and enthroned – the finest present she could give her friend.

Over time, these video evenings had become very important in Jonna and Mari's lives. When the films were over, they talked about them, earnestly and in detail. Jonna put the cassette into a slipcover decorated in advance with text and pictures, copies from the film library she'd been collecting all her life, and the cassette was given its dedicated place on the shelves reserved for videos – an attractive, continuous surface of gold and soft colours with little flags on the backs showing the country where each film was made. Only very rarely did Jonna and Mari have time to see their films a second time. There was an uninterrupted flood of new ones to accommodate. They had long since filled every shelf in the house. The shelves in the hall were in fact badly needed.

Especially close to Jonna's heart were the silent films in black-and-white; Chaplin, in particular, of course. Patiently, she taught Mari to understand the classics. She talked about her student years abroad, the cinema clubs, her rapture at seeing these films, sometimes several a day.

"You understand, I was possessed. I was happy. And now when I see them again, these classics, so awkwardly expressive, with the clumsy technology that was all they had, it's like being young again."

"But you never grew up," said Mari innocently.

"Don't be smart. They're the real thing, those old films. The people who made them went all out, defied their limits. They're hopeful films – young, courageous films."

Jonna also collected what she called "pure movies" – Westerns, Robin Hood films, wild pirate romances, and a lot of other simple stories of justice, courage and chivalry. They stood alongside the films of contemporary multifaceted geniuses and defended their territory. Their slipcovers were blue.

Jonna and Mari sat in their separate chairs in the darkened room and waited for Fassbinder.

"Before I go to sleep," Mari said, "you know, I think more about a film you've shown me than I do about all my worries, I mean all the things I've got to do and all the dumb things I've ever done... It's sort of like your movies freed me from myself. I mean, of course it's still me, but I'm not my own responsibility."

"You do get to sleep pretty quickly," Jonna said. "It can't hurt you to not have a bad conscience once in a while for twenty minutes. Or ten. Now you can go and turn it on."

The little red light came on. Fassbinder confronted them in all his exquisite, controlled violence. It was very late when he was done. Jonna switched on the lamp, slipped the cassette into its cover, and put it on the shelf labelled "Fassbinder".

"Mari," she said, "are you unhappy that we don't see people?"

"No, not any more."

"That's good. I mean, if we did see them, what would it be like? Like always, exactly like always. Pointless chatter about inessentials. No composition, no guiding idea. No theme. Isn't that right? We know roughly what everyone will say; we know each other inside out. But here on our videos every remark is significant, nothing is arbitrary. Everything is considered and well formulated."

"All the same," said Mari, "sometimes one of us might say something unexpected, something that didn't fit, something really out of the ordinary that made you sit up and take notice. You know, something irrational."

"Yes, I know. But make no mistake: great directors know all about the irrational. You talk about things that don't fit – they use such things, with a purpose, as an essential part of the whole. Do you know what I mean? Apparent quirkiness but with a point. They know exactly what they're doing."

"But they've had time," Mari objected. "We don't always have time to think, we just live! Of course a filmmaker can depict what you call quirkiness, but it's still just canned. We're in the moment. Maybe I haven't thought this through... Jonna, these films of yours are fantastic, they're perfect. But when we get involved in them as totally as we do, isn't that dangerous?"

"How do you mean, dangerous?"

"Doesn't it diminish other things?"

"No. Really good films don't diminish anything, they don't close things off. On the contrary, they open up new insights, they make new thoughts thinkable. They crowd us, they deflate our slovenly lifestyle, our thoughtless way of chattering and pissing away our time and energy and passion. Believe me, films can teach us a huge amount. And they give us a true picture of the way life is."

Mari laughed. "Of our slovenly lifestyle, you mean? You mean, maybe they can teach us to piss our lives away with a little more intelligence, a little more elegance?"

"Don't be an ass. You know perfectly well..."

Mari interrupted. "And if film is some kind of edifying god, wouldn't it be dangerous to try and emulate your gods, always knowing that you're coming up short? That everything you do is somehow badly directed?"

The telephone rang and Jonna went to answer it. She listened for a long time, then she said, "Wait a minute, I'll give you his number. Stay calm, it'll just take a second." Mari heard her finish the conversation. "Call back if there's any news. Bye."

"What's happened?" Mari said.

"That was Alma again. Her cat jumped out the window. It was trying to catch a pigeon."

"You're not serious! Mosse? I didn't realise; you were so short with her…"

"I gave her the number for the vet," Jonna said. "You have to be short and matter-of-fact about accidents. You were talking about badly directed."

"Not now!" Mari burst out impatiently. "Their Mosse… Jonna, I think I'll go to bed."

"No," Jonna said. "We have to wait. She might call again and need comfort. You have to answer and talk to her for a while. You know, share it out fair and square." She hung the silver cloth over the television set to protect it from dust and morning sun, and lit the last cigarette of the day.

The Hunter

THE SKERRY WAS SHAPED LIKE AN ATOLL – granite surrounding a shallow lagoon or tidal pool with a narrow passage out to the sea. At low water, the lagoon became a lake. Seals had played there in the old days, before they were shot or moved on to quieter locations. Now eider hens used it for a nursery. The cottage stood on one side of the lagoon; the other side was sea-bird territory. Guano streaked the granite like snow, and white as snow were the nesting gulls and terns and the long, showy borders of daisies in every rocky crevice.

On the highest outcropping, a black-backed gull with a single chick had taken up residence, a huge bird with black wing feathers and a beak like a bird of prey. Their distinct separation from the rest of the settlement seemed to express superiority, contempt. Now and then, as if in distraction, the gull would make its way down the mountain to devour an eider chick. Hundreds of screaming birds would rise in a cloud each time and, one by one, dive steeply on the gull – but never come too close. And the lord of the island would snap at them absent-mindedly and return to his own territory, where he would stand stock-still, distinguished, statuesque on the atoll's highest point.

Jonna liked eider chicks, especially after one of them wandered up to the cottage and insisted on following her. Finally she got the chick into a basket and rowed around for an hour before spotting a likely eider family, distant enough from the territory of the black-backed gulls. "Some day I'll murder those black-backed gulls," she said. "You just can't work in peace around here with all these stupid birds."

One morning, Jonna was oiling her pistol out on the granite slope when, almost without thinking, she fired off a shot across the lagoon in the direction of the gull's stolid silhouette. Whether it was to scare him or to shoot him is uncertain. In any case, the bird collapsed and fluttered down from its mountain top. Mari hadn't seen it, and she was used to hearing Jonna shoot at tin cans. Jonna went to finish off the bird. She was very upset, but at the same time proud of her marksmanship – it was at least a hundred metres across the lagoon. But the gull was nowhere to be found.

Two days later, Mari came running across the rock. "Jonna," she called, "it can't fly and it can't walk, and the chick doesn't know where to go!"

When they came to the water, the whole shoreline was empty.

But the dismal morning inevitably came when Mari found the black-backed gull dead on the rocks, and by then it was full of worms.

"Typical," Jonna said. "Of course you had to be the one to find it. Well, okay, I'm sorry. I shot it." And she added, "At a hundred metres."

"I might have known," Mari burst out. "I should have guessed! You've killed the King. He was awful, but he belonged to the island, to us! You just love guns! You just can't stop! So now you can take the feathers. Take them. Go ahead, take them! They're just what you need for your blessed graphic acid bath, aren't they?"

"I didn't mean to," Jonna began, but Mari interrupted and began speculating cruelly, thoughtlessly, about when the chick would eventually float ashore. Then she went down to the live-box and put on a demonstration by slaughtering perch, a job she despised and generally left completely to Jonna.

Jonna detached the long pinions, washed and dried them and put them in her work drawer, farthest in. All day she waited for the unavoidable sequel, but it was not until they had laid out their nets that Mari began talking about the concept of the hunter. Somewhere she'd read that people could be broadly divided into hunters, gardeners and fishermen. "The hunter type", she explained, "is naturally the most admired. He's considered to be bold and a little dangerous. You know, a person who plays for high stakes, who can be ruthless and take chances that other people don't dare take. Isn't that right?"

Jonna went on whittling on her net peg, observing by and by that "There must be all kinds, but mostly people are a mixture of all three. Or all ninety-five, or whatever."

"Yes, of course, but there are still typical cases of what we might call hunters. And they're born that way."

"Speaking of gulls," Jonna said, "do you remember the one that broke its wing and crawled to the steps every day? I suppose you were being a gardener when you tried to comfort it with food it didn't even have the strength to eat. And what happened? I threw the pike net over the poor thing's head when you were off doing something else and took care of it quickly with a hammer. I'm sure it was full of worms. You can't mend what's totally broken. And for that matter, you were relieved. You admired me. You said so."

"Well, yes," Mari admitted, "but that was completely different. That's anecdotal evidence."

"There are times," Jonna went on without listening, "there are times when a healthy ruthlessness is the right thing. What about that time those idiots came ashore in their horrible plastic boat – it was purple – and were going to shoot our birds before the season even opened?! And what's more they were drunk, though that doesn't excuse them. Remember?"

"Yes, I remember."

"So you see what I mean. I went down to the shore and gave them a piece of my mind. No effect. They sneered at me and sauntered up onto the island with their shotguns."

"They were dreadful," Mari agreed.

"They were. And then I thought, the only right and just thing to do right now is to shoot holes in their boat. That would teach them, right? A couple of holes at the waterline, bang."

"But how did they get home?!" Mari burst out.

"They had to bale. Or maybe they had rags."

Jonna and Mari sat silent for a moment.

"Odd," Mari said. "Did you say that was last year?"

"Yes. Or the year before. And the boat was violet. Lilac."

"But are you absolutely sure you really shot holes in it, or did you just think about it?"

Jonna stood up and shoved the dinner dishes into the box under the bed. "Maybe I just thought about it," she said then. "But the point ought to be clear enough. You have to realize that there always has to be an aggressor. Someone who attacks when no one else has the guts to get involved. To protect..."

"Ha!" Mari cried. "You're very clever at getting me to go along with all sorts of things that are beside the point! The point is, you think guns are fun! Admit you think they're fun! At midsummer you shot the stovepipe on the tent sauna full of holes, and the smoke's been coming in ever since. Did I say a word about it? No. But let me tell you something once and for all: I loathe that pistol!"

Mari took the rubbish bin and went outside.

After a while, she came back.

"Jonna, they're here again. The purple plastic boat. Can you go down and talk to them?"

"The nerve!" Jonna said. "But maybe they've come to apologize. They might even have brought water. Or wood. Wait. I'll go down and see."

When Jonna was halfway across the meadow, Mari came running after her. "Take this," she said. "You never know." And she handed her the pistol.

Catfishing

THE SUMMER HAD MOVED INTO JUNE. Slowly, thinking Mari didn't notice, Jonna went from window to window, tapped the barometer, walked out on the slope or out on the point, came in again with comments about things that needed attention, complained about the gulls screaming and copulating to drive a person crazy, and spoke her mind about the local radio, which had the most idiotic programmes – for example, about amateurs who had shows and thought they were God's gift to art. And the weather was implacably beautiful the entire time.

Mari said nothing. What could she say?

Finally Jonna got busy. She built up her great unassailable barricade against work, against the agony of work. With small, polished tools she began shaping exquisite small objects of wood, tinier and tinier, more and more beautiful. She visited the islands to the west looking for juniper; she walked the shoreline gathering unusual kinds of driftwood, odd shapes that might give her an idea. She arranged it all on her workbench in symmetrical piles, smaller ones, larger ones, and every piece of sea-polished wood had its own special potential to keep her from making pictures.

One day Jonna was sitting on the granite slope polishing an oval wooden box. She claimed it was an African wood, but she'd forgotten the name.

"Will there be a lid?" Mari asked.

"Of course."

"Have you always worked in wood? I don't mean woodcuts or wood engravings, but for real?"

Jonna put down the wooden box. "For real," she repeated. "That's brilliant. Try to understand, I'm playing. And I mean to go on playing. Do you have a problem with that, maybe?"

The cat came in, sat down, and stared at them.

"Fish," Mari said. "We ought to take in the net."

"And what happens if I do nothing but play? Until I die! What would you say to that?"

The cat meowed angrily.

"And ambition," Mari said. "What are you going to do about your goals?"

"Nothing. Nothing at all."

"But what if you can't help it?"

"I can help it. Don't you understand; there isn't time any more. It's all I do, just observe, observe to distraction, pictures that don't mean shit until I draw them, and redraw them. I've had enough for one life, my only life! And anyway, I don't see them any more. Admit I'm right!"

"Yes," Mari said. "You're right."

The sky had clouded over and there was rain in the air. The cat meowed again.

"Fish," Mari said. "The cat food's all gone."

"We can leave it overnight."

"No. What if the wind picks up? Nothing but seaweed, and it'll catch on the bottom. And you know, it's Uncle Torsten's last net."

"Okay, okay," Jonna said. "Your Uncle Torsten's sacred net that he made when he was ninety."

"Over ninety. We laid it wrong. I know we laid it too close to shore, the bottom there's too rocky."

The cat followed them down to the shore. Jonna rowed and Mari sat in the stern to take up the net. The float had drifted far out behind the point. The wind was rising.

"We're not getting anywhere," Jonna said. "Can't you tell? We're standing still. Your uncle and his blessed net..."

"Be quiet. It was the last thing he did. A little more out, no, no, turn! Backwater a little, backwater... Now I've got it." Mari pulled in line and got hold of the net peg. "Just like I thought, it's hooked on the bottom. Go upwind... Back around. Don't row! Backwater! This is hopeless. And it's his last net."

"Oh, fine," Jonna said. "Wonderful. It won't come up, and if it won't come up then it won't come up. I'll backwater around, all the way around! What do you want?"

Mari was holding the net with both hands and could feel it breaking and tearing apart on the rocks on the seabed. What she'd already gathered slid off the net peg into the bottom of the boat in one big tangle and Jonna shouted, "Let go, let it go!" and the whole thing went back over the gunwale until the net peg stuck up its tail and disappeared. Jonna rowed in against the wind and crashed the bow up on the granite. The cat sat waiting and meowed. They didn't tie up; just climbed out and sat on the thwarts. The sea had turned black to the south. It had begun to blow hard.

"Forget it," said Jonna. "Forget it. Don't grieve for a net, grieve for everything else that's broken and can't ever be mended. Your uncle liked making nets; it was what he knew, it was calming and familiar. Going into that loft you've talked about. I'm sure it helped him shut everything out, and everyone. He wasn't thinking about fish, not a bit, and not about you getting the net as a present. He was just at peace, doing work that was his and only his. You know I'm right. He didn't have goals any more."

"To hell with goals," Mari said. "What I'm talking about is desire, about having to."

"Having to what?"

"I think you know."

"And then what? Those pictures. They drown. They drown and get lost among millions of other pictures. And most of them are completely unnecessary – and, what's more, pretentious." Jonna added a little more quietly, "I mean other people's. Most of them."

The storm came nearer, a huge alien backdrop making its steady way across the water, never before seen in such splendour and maybe never to be repeated. The sky moved toward them in a finely drawn curtain of local thunder showers, each with its own delicate drapery. The light turned subterranean and yellow, the shallows had gone Bengali green. Very soon, it would all be nothing but grey rain.

"Take care of the boat," Jonna shouted, jumping ashore. She ran up to the cottage.

Mari tied up *Viktoria*, two lines on the north side and two on the south. She walked up to the top of the island and saw that the curtain of rain was coming closer, albeit slowly. Jonna would have plenty of time to make her crucial first sketch.

One Time in June

BACK NEAR THE TURN OF THE CENTURY, Mari's mother had helped start the Girl Scouts in Sweden. The girls admired her, of course, but from one very small Scout named Helga she got absolute, unqualified adoration. Helga was as quiet as a mouse and afraid of practically everything. Mari's mother could see that Helga would never under any circumstances become a good scout, and she therefore tried as quietly as possible to protect the child from the simple hardships that might only increase her terror.

Helga's greatest phobia was thunderstorms. When the thunder rolled nearer, Mari's mother would find the unfortunate child and try to calm her with whatever explanations she could come up with – sudden temperature changes, electrical charges, updraughts and downdraughts. It is not certain that Helga understood, but it did make her feel better.

Helga had a camera that she carried wherever her beloved Scout leader took her. She pasted the photographs into a scrapbook that she never showed to anyone. It was her secret treasure, a barricade against a dangerous world. On the first page, she'd pasted in a little lock of hair under cellophane. After a great deal of planning and anxiety, she had clipped off the uttermost tip of her Scout leader's majestic braid.

Remarkably, Helga never looked up her idol after her scouting years, never even sent the inevitable Christmas cards that give the recipient an annual rush of holiday sentimentality or, more often, a twinge of bad conscience. On the other hand, Helga did continue with the Scrapbook, pasting in, as time went by, wedding and birth announcements and everything else that concerned her Friend. The chapter she'd entitled "First and Foremost an Artist" dealt with her participation in art exhibitions and included newspaper reviews, several reproductions and a couple of interviews. The family surrounding her Friend received only that narrow margin of interest that could not be avoided. The Scrapbook ended with an obituary and a poem in which Helga attempted to express all the feelings she had never uttered.

Many years later, Helga happened to see a notice in her morning paper. The early works of several artists were to be auctioned off, and there was a list of names. Helga bought a collection of drawings and watercolours Mari's mother had done during her earliest years as a student. She framed them nicely, hung them, photographed them, and put the pictures in the Scrapbook, which was now complete and perfect.

That summer, for some reason, this perfection came to feel like a burden. Helga decided to shift her protracted responsibility to another altar, and so she wrote to Mari. The material she'd collected was too valuable to send by post, she would have to deliver it in person, and the sooner the better.

Mari read the letter and walked around the island for a while, slowly. When she came back, Jonna said, "We can always sleep in the tent. And it will only be for a couple of days?"

"Yes. I'm sure it'll be only a couple of days."

Brunström's island taxi put Helga ashore on a June evening. She greeted them quietly and solemnly as if at a funeral. Helga was still short, but she had grown in girth. Her face bore an expression of reserved obstinacy. They walked up to the cottage, where a fish soup stood ready on the stove, and had a hard time getting a conversation started. Helga did not want to unpack. "Tomorrow," she said. "Tomorrow is Her birthday."

In the tent, Jonna observed that Helga had brought an awful lot of luggage.

"Yes," Mari said. "Let's read for a while."

The cat came in to go to bed.

The next morning, Helga's Scrapbook lay in the middle of the table. The cover was decorated with a scout emblem in gold. She had lit a candle that burned with an invisible flame in the sunlight.

"Now you should sit down," Helga said. "Mari, here is the book of her life." And she began her narrative. Solemnly, in detail, she told of all the expectations and disappointments she'd experienced in the course of her long, patient effort to give Mari's mother her rightful place in the sacred garden of memory. The photographs were overexposed and faded. Shadowy, barely visible figures did things that evidently mattered to them. But Helga described and explained everything that had occurred.

"Mari, turn to page twenty-three. Did you know that your mother took first prize in block lettering in 1904? I'll read from the school's annual report... Did you know that she was an accomplished marksman? Page twenty-nine. First prize in Stockholm 1908 and second prize in Sundsvall 1907. And did you know that in 1913 she left scouting? And why?"

"I know, "Mari answered. "It had become over-organised and she was tired of it all."

"No, no. She wasn't tired. She surrendered her mantle in order to devote herself entirely to Art. Turn to page forty-five..."

"Excuse me," Jonna said. "I think I'll go out for a while and feed the cat. Wouldn't you like some coffee?"

"No, thank you," Helga said. "This is too important."

A little while later, Mari came rushing out of the cottage. "Did you hear that?" she cried. "The sacred garden of memory! Did you know that my mother had the second-longest hair in Sweden in 1908! That little lock of hair in cellophane makes me sick. She has no right to it!"

"Stop," Jonna said. "You know what I think? I think you should ask her if you can't read the rest of that book by yourself, alone. Say it nicely, don't sound annoyed. Tell her it's personal and important for you, and then you can go out to the end of the point and she can't tell if you're reading it or not."

"Of course I'll read it!" Mari burst out. "I can't not! And why is it any business of yours anyway?"

Jonna said, "Two people on an island can manage, even when things get bad. But three is worse. Mari, she's not trying to steal your mother. Listen to what I'm saying."

Mari took Helga's scrapbook out to the end of the point. It was fine, warm weather with a light breeze from the water.

When Jonna went back to the cottage, Helga had unpacked. All the drawings and watercolours Mari's mother had done as a student were lined up against the walls.

"Don't say anything," Helga said. "It's a surprise. Wait till Mari comes back."

They waited a long time.

Finally Jonna went out and rang the big ship's bell that was only used when danger threatened. Mari came running, threw open the door, and stood stock-still. The sun glistened on all the pretty gold frames. Helga watched her intently.

Eventually Jonna said, carefully, "Of course she was very young."

"Yes," said Helga. "Yes, she was. It's a precious heritage to pass along."

They took down their maps from the walls and put up Mari's mother instead.

"Now we really ought to have a drink," Jonna said. "Don't you think, Mari?"

"Yes. A strong one. But we don't have anything."

And just then the whole cabin shook from a long series of explosions. One watercolour fell to the floor and the glass broke.

"Is it the Russians?" Helga whispered.

"Very likely," Mari said. "We're not so very far from the other side..."

Jonna cut her off. "Now don't be mean! Helga, it's just the military having a little target practice. Nothing to worry about. Do you want to go out and watch?"

Helga shook her head; she was pale.

Out on the slope, Mari said, "She's afraid."

"Don't look so pleased. Do we have enough cat food for a week?"

"No, we don't. But the cat won't eat a minnow as long as this is going on."

"There they go again."

"Oh, I know it by heart," Mari said. "'The Defence Department has issued the following warning: 'Heavy artillery exercise with live ammunition to commence such and such a time and date in such and such an area, danger in five-kilometre sector, height 2000 metres, local populations take heed, blah blah.' And she was leaving tomorrow!"

"I know, I know," Jonna burst out. "It's my fault. I was supposed to get new batteries for the radio and I forgot."

A little tug toiled slowly out to sea towing a gigantic target. White pillars of water rose where shells landed.

"They're not very good shots," Mari observed. "Look, that last one almost hit the boat. They need a longer towline."

The target eventually disappeared out to sea behind the point, and now the shells sailed right over the island. They could hear them whistling overhead and ducked each time. It was hard not to.

"Childish," Mari said. "I think they're actually having fun."

"Not at all. You don't understand. They have to learn to shoot. That's more important than all the fishermen in the world and all the summer people in their little rowboats. It's serious stuff. To put it simply, the military is there to defend us and we ought to do all we can to help and understand. They usually bring in eight hundred men for these manoeuvres. That tells you something."

"Ha," Mari said. "What it tells me is that right now nine hundred eiders are sitting on their eggs!"

And suddenly, with the obviousness of the unexpected, a pillar of water rose just at the edge of their beach, very tall and white. A shell struck the granite and a rain of shrapnel flew across the vegetable garden. They went into the cottage.

"Now listen to me," Jonna said. "We have to take this the right way. Those boys are very young and they aren't very good shots. The target moves behind the island. Okay, so they shoot over the island, but judging distance is very difficult in the beginning. We have to understand that." She put out the coffee cups and moved Helga's scrapbook to one side.

"Give it to me!" Helga shouted. And Mari said, "You can save it in the cellar, and maybe you'd better go down there yourself. Things up here will probably just get worse and worse."

"You're not a bit like your mother!" Helga exclaimed.

"No. I'm not. You ought to know that, since you knew her inside out!"

"Now that's enough," Jonna said. "Put the scrapbook under the mattress and settle down."

The artillery continued until evening, then went quiet. Mari went out with a can of paint and painted white rings around each shell hole. "Something to show people," she explained. "It'll make an impression."

"On whom?"

"Maybe little boys from Viken…"

"Mari, you haven't been especially nice today."

"No. I know."

"Can't you just let it go?"

"She doesn't own her."

"Well," said Jonna, "the worst part, actually, is that those pictures from her student days don't do your mother justice. To put it mildly."

And so the week went on as best it might. At night, the coastal forces trained with searchlights, sweeping the sea. The cold, clinical light rotated regularly through the cabin windows, and no curtains could shut it out. Helga wept.

"Mari, you'll have to move into the cottage," Jonna said. "It'll make her feel better."

"Can't you?"

"No. I'll stay in the tent with the cat. This is something you're going to have to deal with yourself, for once."

Mari dragged her mattress up to the cottage and turned toward the wall to sleep.

It was the last night of artillery manoeuvres, and there was a thunderstorm with hard rain and wind. Helga leaped out of bed and shook Mari awake. "Now they're shooting right at us!" she shouted. "Should we go down to the cellar?"

"No, no, they're not shooting, that's thunder. It's just God shooting at us." Mari lit the lamp and saw that Helga was now seriously frightened. She had never seen a face so terrified. The thunderstorm was directly overhead, the lighting and thunderclaps came simultaneously and the military's blue searchlights were obliterated by the red doomsday illumination of the storm. Fantastic, actually.

"They're not shooting," Mari repeated. "It's just thunder. Go to bed."

"Ball lightning!" Helga cried. "They come in and roll into you, they find you, they roll into you!"

Mari took Helga by the shoulders and shook her. "Quiet!" she said. "Be quiet! Go to bed. Look, I'm closing the damper. Now they can't come in. Look here, put on these rubber boots. Then you'll be safe. Absolutely."

Helga pulled on the rubber boots.

"And now, now I want to explain to you that thunder is a very simple phenomenon... It's all a question of..."

And suddenly Mari couldn't remember exactly how her mother used to explain the thunder away and make it seem natural. She said, a little vaguely, "Something about updraughts..."

Lightning in all four windows, another divine wallop of thunder, and Helga threw herself into Mari's arms and held on as hard as she could. "Yes, yes," she said, "updraughts, right? And downdraughts... And what else? Explain it to me!"

"Electricity," Mari whispered. "It's just simple electricity, that's all..."

The thunderstorm moved north, as always. When thunderstorms come to the islands, they always come from the south and move north; that's common knowledge. Farther and farther away until they can barely be heard, and then it's only the rain.

Mari's arms were going numb from holding Helga. The lamp had starting smoking. "It's over now," she said. "Now you can go to bed, we're out of danger. Listen to me, my friend, we're out of danger now..." It was quite a while before Mari realized that Helga had fallen asleep.

The next morning, after raining all night, the sea was like glass and the island was washed and green. The cat came and cried for food.

They drove to the mainland with Helga and set two nets on the way.

Just before the bus left, Helga turned to Mari and said, "One thing you have to admit. You don't know much about thunderstorms."

"No," Mari answered. "But I'll try to find out."

They pulled up their nets on the way home. One miserable roach and a little bullhead that they set free. The cat stood waiting on the shore.

"It's gone so quiet," Jonna said. "What did you think? Wasn't that a good storm?"

"Very good," Mari said. "The best we've had."

Fog

THEY WERE RIGHT IN THE MIDDLE OF THE SEA-LANE when the fog rolled in, ice cold and yellow. It came quickly. Jonna drove on for a bit, but pretty soon she turned off the motor.

"It's not worth it. We'll miss the island and wind up in Estonia somewhere."

There is no silence like sitting in a fog at sea and listening. Large boats can loom up suddenly, and you don't hear their bow water in time to start your motor and get out of the way. They ought to use their foghorns...

I should have brought my compass, Jonna thought. Dead calm, no help from wind direction. No watch, of course. I didn't even listen to the weather report... And now there she sits, freezing.

"Row a little," she said. "It'll warm you up."

Mari put the oars in the locks. She looked miserable with her narrow, anxious neck and damp hair in tufts over her eyes.

"You're pulling too hard on the right; we're going in circles. But maybe it's just as well."

"Jonna," Mari said, "have you got crispbread in the stern box?"

"No, I don't."

"My mother..." Mari began.

"I know, I know. Your mother always had crispbread with her when she went out to sea. But the fact is, I don't have any crispbread in the stern box."

"Why are you angry?" Mari asked.

"I'm not angry. Why would I be angry?"

A vertical tunnel opened directly above them, leading up to an annoyingly blue summer sky – like flying, except then the tunnel goes straight down.

Finally a ship's foghorn, a long way off.

"Crispbread," Jonna said. "Crispbread, for heaven's sake. Your mother was really fussy about crispbread. She broke it in tiny little pieces and put them in a row and spread butter on each little piece. It took forever. And I had to wait and wait for the butter knife, and she did the same thing every single morning and every day and every year she lived with us!"

Mari said, "You could have had two butter knives."

A gigantic shadow rose up from the fog and glided past like a wall of darkness. Jonna yanked the motor to life and raced away and turned it off.

Gradually the wake died, and it became completely still.

"Were you scared?" Jonna said.

"No. I didn't have time. Incidentally," Mari went on, "your mother was pretty fussy about baking bread. She was always sending us loaves of her bread and every time she sent them off, she'd call at seven in the morning and talk for an hour. Graham bread. When it got mouldy we used to call it Graham Green."

"Ha ha, so amusing," Jonna said. "And speaking of mothers, your mother used to cheat at poker."

"That's possible. But she was eighty-five years old!"

"No, she was eighty-eight when she cheated. Don't deny it."

"Okay, fine, she was eighty-eight. But at that age you've got the right to do certain things."

"Never," said Jonna solemnly. "At that age a person should have learned to respect her opponent. Your mother cheated shamelessly, and you might as well admit it. She didn't take me seriously, and you have to in a serious game. Row a little harder on the left."

It had grown really cold. The fog drifted over them, through them, as impenetrable as ever. Jonna took the dibbling hooks out of the stern box. They might just as well dibble for cod if the day was ruined anyway. But somehow they didn't feel like dibbling.

They just waited.

"Funny," Mari said. "Sitting here this way, you start thinking about all sorts of things. What time is it?"

"We don't have a watch. Or a compass."

"That stuff about our mothers," Mari went on. "There's something I've never dared ask. Jonna, what did you two fight about, really? Mother might say the wind was blowing from the northwest, and right away you'd say it was straight from the north. Or north-northwest, or south-northeast, you'd go on like that. And I knew that deep down you were fighting about completely different things. Important, dangerous things!"

"Of course we were," Jonna said.

Mari stopped rowing. Very slowly she said, "Really? Don't you think it's finally time to let me in on what it was you were fighting about? Be honest. We need to talk about it."

"Fine," Jonna said. "Terrific. Then what you need to know is that your mother, the whole time, year after year, was secretly swiping my tools. She ruined one knife after another – she didn't know how to sharpen them. And let's not even talk about chisels! Don't even talk to me about all the precision tools that you carry with you half your life, tools you get to know and love – and then someone comes along who doesn't get it, doesn't respect them, someone who handles your delicate instruments like they were can openers! Yes, yes, I know what you're going to say. Her little ships were wonderful, and beautifully made, but why couldn't she have bought her own tools? She could have wrecked those to her heart's content!"

Mari said, "Yes. That was bad. Very bad." She starting rowing again, and after a while she raised the oars out of the water to say, "It was your fault she stopped making ships."

"What do you mean?"

"She saw that yours were better."

"And now you're angry?"

"Don't be an ass," Mari said and started to row again. "Sometimes you make me crazy."

They hadn't noticed the fog moving off. The heavy summer fog had rolled on north to annoy people on the inner islands, and suddenly the sea was open and blue and they found themselves a long way out toward Estonia. Jonna started the motor. They came back to the island from a totally new direction, and it didn't look the same.

Killing George

WHEN MARI CAME INTO THE FRONT HALL, she heard the printing press working.

"Are you here again?" Jonna said from inside her studio.

"I just came for those pens..."

Jonna lifted her print and studied it severely. "No," she said. "I know you've brought your George. You've changed him."

"Yes. The whole ending. The whole idea! I've got rid of a lot of repetitions, and Stefan isn't called Sveffe any more. His name is Kalle."

"Good heavens," Jonna said.

"Maybe I should come back a little later?"

"No, no, sit down somewhere. I'll finish this tomorrow."

They sat across from each other at the window table. Jonna lit a cigarette and said, "You don't need to take it from the beginning. I know that part. 'Miss, another round', and so on. Anton went out to use the phone. Take it from the turtle."

"But you know I have to take it from the beginning or it won't be whole! Could I read it fast up to where it's new? That part when they go to the restaurant is out, and no pointless explanations about Anton, he's just there. By the way, do you really believe in this idea?"

"Absolutely. But maybe it's not enough, not really. It may be difficult to finish."

"But I've come to the end!"

Jonna said, "Anyway, take it from the turtle." And Mari put on her glasses.

'Speaking of sad things,' Kalle said, 'did you read that piece about the lonely turtle in the paper the other day? Its name is George.'

'No, what about it?'

'The interesting thing about this turtle is that it's the last of its kind, Galapagos or something. He's the absolute last one of his particular turtle species, and after him there are no more.'

'I'll be damned,' said Bosse.

'Yes. And he walks in a circle, around and around, searching.'

'How do they know he walks in a circle?'

'They have him in a cage,' Kalle explained. 'He's under constant observation. George. He's searching for a female, you see.'

'And how do they know that?'

'They're pretty sure about it. Scientists, you know.'

'Okay,' said Bosse. 'And your point of course is that Anton's doing the same thing, phoning and phoning and no one ever answers. Should we go look for him?'

"Wait a minute," Jonna said. "This Anton. He's forever going out to use the phone. The woman never answers. Why does he have to keep calling her? I mean, if she doesn't answer, she's just not home. And I think your parallel with the turtle is far-fetched, although you know I have nothing against turtles..."

"Exactly," Mari burst out. "Good. You like the turtle, but you don't like the rest of it! But I told you, I've changed the whole ending, totally!"

"Read on," Jonna said.

'You know, Bosse, sometimes I get so damned depressed.'

'You do?'

'Yes, it's all so pointless.'

'But what can you do about it? That George... How can they know there's not another one, how can they be sure?'

'They just know,' Kalle said. 'They've looked everywhere.'

'But I don't think they've searched enough. They can't have had time to search the whole earth, every damned little place, and then try to tell us that... Look, I'm tired of your George.'

'Fine, forget it. I'm sorry I brought him up. Miss, another round.'

"Stop," Jonna said. "Are you sure you haven't made these men a little too simple?"

"They are simple," Mari answered. "Now Anton comes in:

'Look,' said Kalle, 'we saved your drinks. Now you've got two.'

'Nice of you,' said Anton.

Bosse said, 'No answer?'

'No. But I mean to keep trying.'

"How many times does he call, this Anton?" Jonna asked. "And what does he look like? What does he do, who is he? Never mind. Jump to 'I don't know if it's dreadful or a comfort.' I like that."

Mari read.

When Anton had gone, Kalle looked Bosse in the eye and said, 'But anyway, those scientists are really fantastic, aren't they? I mean, they don't give up trying to find George a wife. Even though she doesn't exist. For that matter, wouldn't it be worse if she did exist but they never found her?' He emptied his glass gravely and added, 'I don't know if it's dreadful or a comfort.'

"Here I cut half a page."

'Bosse, do you know what makes me so tired, so very unhappy? It's that nothing fits. Listen to me. It's as if nothing mattered. Like, secretly. You never know why and how things have happened. Nothing fits together. Do you know what I mean?'

"Bosse said, 'And why should it fit together? In what way? What did you expect?'

'Some sort of meaning to it all.'

"Stop," Jonna said. "You said that earlier. You're going on and on about it. What is it you're after? As far as I remember..."

Mari ripped off her glasses and shouted, "But I've changed the whole ending! I told you! Do you want to know what I've done? The woman he's calling doesn't exist. She doesn't exist! Anton's calling his own number! Calling himself, you see? Isn't that better?"

"Yes," Jonna said.

"Okay. You agree that makes it better. Now he comes back to the table, and Bosse and Kalle can see that something has happened. I'll read..."

"Wait a second," Jonna said. "Tell me what you're thinking."

"I'm killing her," Mari explained. "That is to say, Anton's killing her. So he doesn't have to go on phoning. Bosse and Kalle are upset, of course, and they order more drinks to comfort him..."

"I don't think you should use more drinks," Jonna said. "But that's a good idea with the woman. What about doing away with George as well? I mean, it's just a thought."

"But you like him," Mari said. "You said he was good." She stood up and gathered her papers. "This isn't going to work."

"Yes it will," Jonna said. "You just need to rewrite it another way. Shall we have some coffee?"

"No. I don't think I want any coffee."

"Mari. We've got Kalle's melancholy conclusion that nothing matters. We've got George who just goes around in circles and doesn't know it's hopeless. But then we've got Anton who dares to kill a lie. It's Anton who might be interesting, and you don't care about him at all. Forget George and think about Anton. Why is he behaving this way? Your engine's idling and you need to add a little fresh insanity, and now I'm going to make coffee."

Jonna filled the teakettle in the bathroom. Looking in the mirror, looking at her own face, she thought with sudden bitterness that it couldn't go on like this, these short stories that were never finished and just went on and on getting rewritten and discarded and picked up again, all those words that got changed and changed places and I can't remember how they were yesterday and what's happened to them today! I'm tired! I'll go in and tell her, now, right now... For example, I wonder if she could describe me well enough to give people a quick, convincing picture. What could she say? A broad, inhospitable face, lots of wrinkles, brown hair going grey, large nose?

Jonna took in the coffee and said, "Try to describe what I look like."

"Seriously?"

"Yes."

"Just half a cup," Mari said. "I think I'll head home." After a while, she said, "I'd try to describe a kind of patience. And stubbornness. Somehow bring out the fact that you don't want anything except... well, except what you want. Wait a moment... Your hair has an unusual hint of bronze, especially against the light. Your profile and your short neck make one think of, you know, old Roman emperors who thought they were God himself... Wait. It's the way you move and the way you walk. And when you slowly turn your face toward me. Your eyes..."

"One of them's grey and the other one's blue," Jonna said. "And now drink your coffee because you need to stay alert. We'll take the whole thing from the beginning. Read slowly, we've got time. Concentrate on Anton, always Anton. He has to come alive. You can sacrifice even George if you have to. Read slowly. *Kalle says, 'Miss, another round.'* Real slow. We need to pay attention. Every time it seems wrong, we stop. Every time we get something like an idea, we'll stop. Are you ready? Read."

Travels with a Konica

JONNA MADE MOVIES. She'd acquired an 8mm Konica, and she loved the small device and took it with her everywhere they traveled.

"Mari," she said, "I'm tired of static pictures. I want to make pictures that are alive. I want motion, change. You know what I mean: everything happens just once and right now... My film is my sketchbook. Look at that! There comes the commedia dell'arte!"

And there they came, street performers with their plush rug, the child on the ball, the strong man who could swallow fire, the girl juggler. People stopped on the street and moved closer to the show. It was very hot. The light flickered and the shadows were a sharp dark blue.

Mari stood close beside Jonna with an opened Kodak film in her hand. She was waiting for the camera's steady whirring to change speed, at which point she had to have a new roll ready instantly. Another important job was keeping Jonna's field of view open. Mari saw it as a point of honour to keep people from walking in front of the camera.

"Don't worry about them," Jonna said. "They're just extras. I'll clip them out."

But Mari said, "Let me. It's my job."

Equally important was finding Kodak film. And Mari searched. In the cities, the towns, at bus stops, she kept an eye out for the gold-and-red sign showing that here you could buy Kodak. Agfa seemed to be everywhere.

"It comes out blue-green," Mari said. "Wait. I'll find Kodak." And she'd search on, all the while afraid that they'd encounter something fantastic – one of those never-to-be-repeated street events that would play out before their eyes just as the film ran out – and then have to wander on trying to forget what they'd lost.

They travelled from city to city, Jonna, Mari and Konica. Mari grew critical. She began giving instructions and advice and involved herself in questions of composition and lighting and bustled about looking for suitable subjects.

They arrived at the Great Aquarium, at the dolphins' turquoise tank, and Mari grabbed Jonna by the arm and yelled, "Wait, I'll tell you when it's going to jump. You're wasting film..." And the dolphin corkscrewed high out of the water, sparkling in the sun, and Jonna burst out, "Now I missed it! Let me decide for myself!"

"By all means!" Mari said. "You and your Konica."

It was inconceivably beautiful and mysterious down in the dark passages where the tank was lit underground. The whales were diving. Through the glass walls you could see the power of their dance as they plunged downward and turned and shot up into the light again. "It's too dark," Mari said. "You won't get anything; the film will just be black…"

"Quiet!" Jonna said. "The shark's coming."

People pushed forward to see the monster, and Mari threw her arms wide to stop them. The shark came; a slow, grey shadow swept past close to the glass and vanished.

"Good," said Jonna. "I got it. You've always wanted to see a real shark up close. Now you have."

Mari said, "I didn't see it."

"What do you mean, didn't see it?"

"I was only thinking of the Konica! I'm always thinking about the Konica and not about what I see! It just goes by."

"But don't be angry." Jonna held out her camera in both hands. "Your shark is here, it's in here! When we get home you can see it as many times as you want, whenever you want. And with music."

Nothing made Jonna happier than finding a circus, or maybe even better a Sunday carnival somewhere on a city's outskirts. They searched one out with the Konica, heard at a distance the breathless staccato of the carousel. Jonna started her tape recorder. "We'll start here," she whispered. "We'll get closer and closer, quite slowly – anticipation. And our footsteps. Then the visual."

They never rode the carousel.

And later, a long time later, in her studio, Jonna set up the screen, focused the projector, and turned off the ceiling light. Mari sat waiting with pen and paper. The machine began to whir and threw a rectangle of light across the screen.

"Makes notes where I should cut," Jonna said. "And the repeats."

"Yes, yes, I know. And when it goes black."

Their trip came toward them. Mari made notes:

head gone to r.

jumping

fence on l.

too long beach

unnec. landsc.

people gone too fast

flower blurred

She wrote and wrote, and afterwards she didn't really know where they had been.

"The clipping is even harder than the filming," Jonna explained. "When I've cut it, we can add music, but not yet. Music makes you uncritical."

"Jonna, right now I want to see something with music. And without taking notes."

"What do you want to see?"

"Mexico. The empty carnival. You know, all the people who were too poor to ride the carousel."

Jonna put in the cassette, an endless, mournful marimba. The picture was blurry and shaky at first but gathered itself suddenly into a long, evening landscape –

the empty field outside Mazatlán. There was the drainage ditch running out toward the ocean, reflecting a last glimpse of the sunset in a long band of burning gold that quickly died. Then the barracks, the car dump, and now, far off, the Ferris wheel with its many-coloured lights that rose and sank and rose and sank.

The Konica came closer and you could see that all the little pleasure boats were empty. The picture moved over to a carousel that was also revolving and just as empty. Everything was sparkling and tempting and ready for fun, but the people strolling slowly through the carnival took no part in the amusements; they just observed. Except for some boys shooting at targets, whose stern faces Jonna had caught in a close-up.

As the film went on, dusk sank deeper over Mazatlán, the people left, but the Ferris wheel kept on turning, now just a circle of rising and falling lights. It was almost night. The marimba played on. The back of the circus tent, indistinct, some dogs rooting around in a rubbish tip.

"Terrible," Mari said. "Terribly good. All those people who just had to go home without... But at least they saw it, didn't they? Didn't you get the ditch at the end, too? That sparkled?"

"Wait, it's coming."

The picture went black and stayed black for a long time. Several weak flashes of light, nothing more, and the screen was empty.

Mari said, "You have to cut that; no one will get it. It was too dark."

Jonna turned off the projector and turned on the overhead light. She said, "Right there it has to be absolutely black, graphically black. But you were there now, weren't you?"

"Yes," Mari answered. "I was there."

B-Western

JONNA CAME IN WITH A BOTTLE OF BOURBON, a carafe of water, and a packet of Cortez cigarillos.

"Aha," said Mari, "the Wild West. A B-Western?"

"Yes. An early classic."

The room was cold, and Mari wrapped herself in a blanket. "What time?"

"Actually," Jonna said. "Actually, it would probably be better if I watched it alone."

"I promise not to say a word."

"Yes, but I'll know what you're thinking, and I can't concentrate." Jonna poured them both a drink. "You think Westerns repeat the same theme over and over. That may be. But you have to understand that Americans are in love with their history, which was so short and powerful, and they describe and depict it again and again... Are you in love with the Renaissance? What do you care about the ancient Egyptians? The Chinese?"

"Not much," Mari said. "They're just there. Or were."

"Fine. Now don't assume that I'm defending B-Westerns, but think about it, try to imagine what it was like in the early days. Courage! Courage and patience. And pure curiosity. Imagine being among the very first to discover and conquer a new country, a new continent!"

"Conquer," Mari repeated and pulled the blanket tighter.

"Yes, yes. Now don't go on about the Indians and all that stuff about cruelty and arrogance; those things happen on both sides. Great change always involves great intensity. That's just the way it is, right? Look at their desolate little towns in a completely empty landscape, and remember they lived in constant danger... They had to develop a strict, an implacable, sense of justice, they had to try to invent the Law for themselves, as best they could..." Jonna put down her cigarillo. "It doesn't draw," she said. "It's the wrong kind."

Mari remarked that perhaps the cigarillos had been lying around too long, and Jonna went on. "It must be that lawlessness has its own laws. Of course mistakes occurred. They lived such violent lives that they simply didn't have time to reflect, that's what I think. But mistakes happen today, too, don't they? We hang the wrong guy, so to speak."

Jonna leaned forward and looked at her friend earnestly. "The sense of honour," she announced. "Believe me, the sense of honour has never been so strong. Friendship between men. You said the heroines were idiotic. Fine, they are idiotic. But take them away, forget them, and what do you find? Friendship between men who are unswervingly honourable toward one another. That's the concept of the Western."

"I know," Mari said. "They have an honourable fist fight and then they're friends for life. Unless the noblest of them gets shot at the end, sacrificing his life to soft music."

"Now you're just being mean," said Jonna. She lifted aside the cloth that protected her television screen and turned to channel two.

"Anyway, I'm right," Mari said. "It's the same thing over and over. They ride past precisely the same mountain and the same waterfall and that Mexican church. And the saloon. And the oxcarts. Don't they ever get tired of it?"

"No," Jonna answered. "They never do. It's about recognition, about recognizing what you've imagined. People make dreams, don't they? The oxcarts that fight their way forward through unexplored territory, dangerous lands... Whether it's an A-Western or a B or even a C, they feel this is the way it must have been, just like this, and it makes them proud and maybe gives them a little comfort. I think."

"Yes," Mari said. "Well, yes, maybe you're right . . ."

But Jonna couldn't stop. "It's not fair of you to come and talk about repetition and the same thing over and over, and anyway your short stories are the same way, the same theme over and over again. Now close the curtains; it starts in three minutes."

Mari dropped the blanket on the floor and announced, very slowly, "I think... now I think I'll go to bed."

She had a hard time falling asleep. Now they're galloping past the red mountain. Now they're playing poker in the saloon. Honky-tonk... They're shooting bottles in the bar, girls are screaming. Now the stairs to the second floor are crashing down...

A trumpet blast woke her up, and she knew the movie had come to the brave men in the final fort. Maybe they've more or less worked things out with the Indians – everyone forgives everyone, except maybe the ones who died – and now they're playing 'My Darling Clementine', which means she's finally figured out who she loved the whole time.

And now Jonna's turning off the television and rewinding the video. She's brushing her teeth and coming to bed and doesn't say a word.

Mari asked, "Was it good?"

"No. But I'm saving it anyway."

"Still, I liked 'My Darling Clementine'," Mari said. "They use that same song every time, but somehow it's right."

Jonna got up and closed the window because the snow had begun to blow in. The room was very peaceful.

Before Mari fell asleep, she asked if they could watch this same B-Western some other evening, and Jonna said yes, she supposed they could.

In the Great City
of Phoenix

AFTER A LONG BUS TRIP THROUGH ARIZONA, Jonna and Mari came late in the evening to the great city of Phoenix and checked into the first hotel they could find near the bus station.

It was called the Majestic, a heavy building from the 1910s with an air of shabby pretension. The lobby with its long mahogany counters beneath dusty potted palms, the broad staircase up to the gloom of the upper floors, the row of stiff, velvet sofas – everything was too grand, everything except the desk clerk, who was tiny under his wreath of white hair. He gave them their room key and a form to fill out and said, "The elevator closes in twenty minutes."

The elevator operator was asleep. He was even older than the desk clerk. He pushed the button for the third floor and sat back down on his velvet chair. The elevator was a huge ornamented bronze cage and it rattled upward very slowly.

Jonna and Mari entered a static, desolate room with way too much furniture and went to bed without unpacking. But they couldn't sleep. They relived the bus trip again and again, through shifting landscapes of desert and snowy mountains, cities without names, white salt lakes, and brief pauses in little towns they knew nothing about and to which they would never return. The trip went on and on, leaving everything behind, hour after hour, a long, long day in a silver-blue Greyhound bus.

"Are you asleep?" Jonna asked.

"No."

"We can get our films developed here. I've been filming blind for a month and haven't any idea what I've got."

"Are you sure it was a good idea to shoot through the bus window? I think we were going too fast."

"I know," Jonna said. And, after a while, "But it was so pretty."

They left the films to be developed, which would take a couple of days.

"Why is the city so empty?" Mari asked.

"Empty?" repeated the man behind the camera counter. "I never thought about it. But I suppose it's because most people live outside of town and drive in to work and then back home."

When Jonna and Mari came back to their room, they noticed a change, a small but sweeping change. It was their first encounter with the invisible chambermaid, Verity. Verity's presence in the hotel room was powerful. It was everywhere. She had reorganized their travellers' lives in her own way. This Verity was an obvious perfectionist and at the same time a conspicuous free spirit. She had laid out Jonna's and Mari's belongings symmetrically but with a certain humour; had unpacked their travel mementos and arranged them on the dresser in a caravan whose placement did not lack irony; had placed their slippers with the noses touching and spread out their nightgowns so the sleeves were holding hands. On their pillows she'd put books she'd found and liked – or perhaps disliked – using their stones from Death Valley as bookmarks. Those ugly stones must have amused her greatly. She had given the room a face.

Jonna said, "Someone's having fun with us."

The next evening, the mirror was decorated with their Indian souvenirs. Verity had washed and ironed everything she thought needed washing and ironing and placed it in symmetrical piles, and in the middle of the table was a large bunch of artificial flowers, which, if they remembered correctly, had previously adorned the lobby.

"I wonder," Mari said. "I wonder if she does this in all the rooms, and is it to cheer up the hotel guests or herself? How does she have the time? Is she just teasing the other chambermaids?"

"We'll see," said Jonna.

They met Verity in the corridor. She was large, with red cheeks and a lot of black hair. She laughed out loud and said, "I'm Verity. Were you surprised?"

"Very much," replied Jonna politely. "We wondered what made you so playful?"

"I thought you looked like fun," Verity said.

And so, quite naturally, they began to be friends with Verity. Every day she was interested to know if Jonna's films had come back. No, they hadn't. It would take a whole week before Jonna and Mari could travel on to Tucson.

Verity was amazed. "Why Tucson, of all places? It's just another town, except it's the closest city on the map. Why do you have to keep travelling, here or there or somewhere else? Is there such a big difference? You've got your health and each other's company. Moreover, now you've got me. For that matter, you should meet the residents. They can be very interesting if you take them the right way."

"The residents?"

"Pensioners, of course. Aren't you pensioners your-selves? Why else would you have come to the Majestic?"

"Nonsense," said Jonna, somewhat sharply, and headed for the stairs.

Verity said, "But aren't you going to take the elevator? Albert likes people to take his elevator. I'm going down myself."

Albert stood up and pressed the button for the ground floor.

"Hi, Albert," said Verity. "How are the legs?"

"The left one's working better," Albert said.

"And how's the birthday coming?"

"I don't know yet. But it's all I think about, all the time."

In the lobby, Verity explained. "Albert's going to be eighty, and he's terribly anxious about his birthday. Should he invite all the residents or just the ones he likes and then the others will be hurt? By the way, would you like to have some fun this evening? Of course everyone goes to bed early at the Majestic..."

"Not us," Jonna said. "But this city is empty and quiet in the evenings. You know that."

Verity looked at her for a moment, almost sternly. "Don't talk like a tourist. I'll take you to Annie's bar. I'll come and get you when I've finished work."

It was a very small bar, long and narrow with a pool table in the back. Annie herself tended the bar, the jukebox played constantly, and people came in steadily and greeted one another in passing as if they'd seen each other an hour ago, which perhaps they had. No ladies among the clientele.

Verity said, "Now you're going to have Annie's banana drink, an Annie Special, her treat. Tell her you like it, then you can get a real drink to chase it. Annie's my friend. She's got two kids and she's a single mother."

"On the house," Annie said. "And where do you come from? Finland? Oh, I didn't think you were allowed to travel to other countries..." She turned her smile toward new customers, but after a while she came back and wanted to give them another Banana Special. They had to toast Finland.

"In that case, Annie, I think we'll need some vodka," Verity said. "Am I right?"

Somebody played the current hit, "A Horse with No Name", and Annie poured vodka into three small glasses, raised a quick, invisible glass of her own, and disappeared to take care of other customers. Jonna opened her tape recorder, and a Stetson to their right hollered, "Hey, Annie! They're stealing our music!"

"They like it!" Annie hollered back. "How did it go with that job?"

"Nothing came of it. How are the kids?"

"Fine. Willy's had a sore throat, so John's bound to catch it. Getting sitters is hopeless."

The bar had grown crowded.

"Give these ladies some space!" Annie yelled. "They're from Finland."

Verity turned to the Stetson and told him cheerfully that her new friends, among other curious undertakings, had travelled a great distance out of the city "in order to see a cactus garden, of all things – cactus that doesn't even flower – and there's an entrance fee!"

"Very bad," said the Stetson sadly. "Pure weeds. I cleaned out a whole patch of them at the Robinsons' last week. They didn't pay much."

"Let me show you something interesting," said their neighbour to the left. "Look, a wonderful little item that ought to sell like nobody's business, but doesn't." He put three small plastic dogs on the bar, one pink, one green, one yellow, and the dogs began marching side by side, the green one in the lead. Mari looked at Jonna, but

Jonna shook her head. It meant, no, he's not trying to sell them, he just wants to amuse us.

The friendly crowding, the jukebox, the pool balls clicking from the curtained-off section of the room, a sudden laugh in the even flood of conversation, a voice being raised to object or explain, and people coming in the whole time and somehow finding space. Annie worked as if possessed but with no trace of nerves, her smile was her own, and the fact that she was hurrying did not mean time was short.

They left the bar and walked back to the hotel. The broad street was empty, and there were lights in only a few windows.

"The cactus garden," Mari said. "That was nothing to laugh at. It was done with great care, with great love! Just sand and more sand, all the plants prickly and grey – they were as tall as statues or so tiny they had to put up barriers so people wouldn't step on them, and everything had its name on a visiting card. It was a brave garden." She added, "Verity, you're brave yourself."

"What do you mean?"

"This city. And the hotel."

"Why do you take everything so seriously?" Verity asked. "Cactuses like sand, they grow, they do all right. Visiting cards, that's dumb! And I'm doing all right myself. At the Majestic I know all the codgers and all their tricks and dodges, and I know Annie, and now I know you. I've got everything I need. And Phoenix is just the place where I happen to live, right? What's so remarkable about that?"

The desk clerk woke up when they came in.

"Verity," he said, "you'll have to take the stairs, you know. But the elevator will be running again tomorrow."

The elevator was decorated with bows of black ribbon. As they were climbing the stairs, Verity explained. "Albert died this afternoon, on the second floor. So we're paying our respects."

"Oh, I'm so sorry," Mari said.

"No need to be sorry. He never had to face that birthday he was so worried about. Jonna, when will your films be ready?"

"Tomorrow."

"And then you're going on to Tucson?"

"Yes."

"There's probably no Annie's bar in Tucson. I've heard unpleasant things about that town, I really have."

In the room, Verity had put all the shoes she could find in marching order toward the door and turned the flower vase upside down. The curtains were drawn, and the suitcase lay open. Verity had been explicit.

Jonna's films were ready the next day. They could see the bus trip across Arizona on the camera store's picture screen, a small device that the owner had placed on the counter for the convenience of tourists. Jonna and Mari watched in silence. It was dreadful. An incoherent, flickering stream of pictures sliced to bits by telephone poles, pine trees, fences. The landscape tipped over and came up straight again and hurried on. It was a mess.

"Thanks," said Jonna. "I think that's enough. I haven't actually had this camera very long."

He smiled at her.

"But the Grand Canyon," Mari said. "Can't we see just a little bit, please?"

And the Grand Canyon made its entrance in the majesty of a fiery dawn. Jonna had held the camera steady and taken time. It was beautiful.

They walked back to the hotel and ran into Verity in the corridor. "Are they good?" she asked at once.

"Very good," Mari said.

"And you're sure you want to go to Tucson tomorrow?"

"Yes."

"Tucson is a horrible place, believe me. There's nothing there to film." Verity turned on her heel and continued down the corridor, calling back over her shoulder, "I'll see you at Annie's this evening!"

Nothing had changed at Annie's bar. The regulars were there and greeted them in a careless, friendly way. They each had a Banana Special on the house. The pool players were hard at it, and the jukebox was playing "The Horse with No Name".

"Business as usual," said Mari and smiled at Verity. But Verity didn't want to talk. The man with the plastic dogs was there. The green, the pink and the yellow had their race across the bar.

"Take them with you," he said. "They're great for making bets when things get slow."

On their way home, Verity said, "I forgot to ask Annie if John caught that sore throat. When does your bus leave?"

"Eight o'clock."

When they came to the Majestic, a fire truck screamed by through the empty streets. It was a windy night, but very warm.

Verity said, "Shall we say goodbye right now and get it over with?"

"Let's do," said Jonna.

In the room, Jonna opened her tape recorder. "Listen to this," she said. "I think it'll be good."

The jukebox through a torrent of people talking, Annie's bright voice, pool balls clicking, the jingle of the cash register – a pause, then their steps on the sidewalk; finally the fire engine and silence.

"But why are you crying?" Jonna said.

"I don't really know. Maybe the fire truck..."

Jonna said, "We'll send a pretty postcard to Verity from Tucson. And one to Annie."

"There aren't any pretty cards of Tucson! It's a dreadful place!"

"We could stay here for a while?"

"No," Mari said. "You can't repeat. It's the wrong ending."

"Of course. Writers," Jonna said and counted out the next day's vitamins into two small glasses.

Wladyslaw

THE SNOW HAD COME EARLY, a blizzard at the end of November. Mari went to the railway station to meet Wladyslaw Leniewicz. His journey from Lodz via Leningrad had been in process for months, with repeated applications, recommendations, and investigations passing slowly from one distrustful office to another. The letters to Mari grew more and more agitated:

"I am brought to despair. Do they not understand, can they not grasp, these cretins, whom they are delaying? The man who has been called The Marionette Master! But, my dear unknown friend, we approach one another, we shall meet despite everything to speak freely of Art's innermost essence. Do not forget my sign of recognition, a red carnation in my buttonhole! Au revoir!"

The train arrived. There he was, one of the first to alight, long and thin in a huge black coat, no hat, his white hair fluttering in the wind. Even without the carnation, Mari would have known that this was Wladyslaw, such an utterly odd bird. But she was surprised at how old he was, really old. All Wladyslaw's letters seemed written with youthful intensity, full of overblown adjectives. Plus his disconcerting penchant for hurt feelings at something she had written or failed to write. He sometimes spoke of her "tone of voice". Mari's tone of voice had been wrong – and she did not give their shared work her undivided attention. Every misunderstanding must be elucidated, analysed in detail, all their intercourse must be clear and pure as crystal! Oh those letters on the hall floor, her name and address in great, bold letters across the entire envelope . . .

"Wladyslaw!" she called. "You are here, you are finally here!"

He crossed the platform with long, elastic strides, carefully put down his valise, and fell on his knees before her in the snow. A very old face, deeply furrowed, with a large protruding nose. And, astonishingly, enormous dark eyes that seemed to have lost nothing of their youthful lustre.

"Wladyslaw, my dear friend," said Mari. "I beg you. Stand up."

He opened a bag and strewed an armful of red carnations at her feet. The wind swept them across the platform and Mari bent down to gather them up.

"No," said Wladyslaw, "let them be. They shall

lie here, a tribute to the Finnish legend, proof that
Wladyslaw Leniewicz passed this way." He rose, picked
up his valise, and offered her his arm.

"Excuse me," said an arriving passenger, a friendly
woman in a fox hat. "Excuse me, but surely you're not
going to leave all those lovely flowers in the snow?"

"I don't really know," Mari answered, terribly
embarrassed. "It's nice of you to ask... But I think we
have to go..."

Mari unlocked her door. "Welcome," she said.

Wladyslaw set down his valise, again very carefully.
He seemed totally uninterested in the room he had just
entered, hardly glancing around. He did not want to
take off his long black coat. "One moment – I must call
my embassy."

It was not a long call, but it was very intense. Mari
heard his disappointment and – before he hung up – an
expression of lofty contempt.

"My dear friend," Wladyslaw said, "you may take my
coat. It will be the case that I remain here, with you."

In the afternoon, Mari ran across the attic to Jonna.
"Jonna, he's arrived, and he's eaten nothing on the
whole trip, and now he doesn't want to eat because he's
too upset. But he said maybe ice cream..."

"Calm down," Jonna said. "Where is he staying?"

"With me. A hotel won't do, he's way too proud. And
he's at least ninety years old and says he prefers to discuss
art at night! He only sleeps a couple of hours!"

"I'm not surprised," Jonna said. "Better and better. Do
you like him?"

"Very much," Mari said.

"Good. I'm going out for food in any case, so I'll get some ice cream and bring it over. And a couple of steaks. He'll probably want something to eat by this evening."

"But don't ring the bell – not yet. Just put it down outside the door. And I'm out of potatoes."

Wladyslaw and Mari ate ice cream and drank tea.

"Tell me about your trip."

"Dreadful," he burst out. "Faces, faces – and their hands! Expressionless, meaningless, raw material I no longer need because I know. I know how to shape a changing countenance to its uttermost expressiveness. I can use simplicity and nuance to make a marionette almost unbearable! You, my precious friend, have drawn certain figures. I beg your forgiveness – but those figures are mute. They do not speak to me. Their hands do not speak to me. But I have given them life, I have taken them over and given them life!"

"Well, well," Mari said. "But then they're not mine any more."

Wladyslaw was not listening. "Theatre, puppet theatre, what do you think it is? Life. Violent life simplified down to its essence, conclusively. Listen to me. I take an idea, the tiniest fragment of an idea, and I think. I feel. And I refine!" He leaped up and began striding back and forth across the room with long, almost dancing steps. "No, say nothing. What is it I have found? I have found a glass shard of what I call the Finnish legend, a shard of a clumsy fairy tale, and I have made this glass shard sparkle like a diamond! Is there any more tea?"

"Not at the moment," Mari replied rather coldly.

"You should use a samovar."

Mari filled the saucepan and turned on the hotplate. "It will take a while," she said.

Wladyslaw said, "I don't like your tone."

"According to the contract," Mari began, conscientiously, and he interrupted her at once.

"You amaze me. Do you speak to me of contracts, of repulsive trivia with which an artist need not concern himself?"

"Now listen to me!" she burst out. "I was supposed to have approval! After all, they're mine, they were mine. And when do I finally get to start making dinner?"

Wladyslaw continued pacing back and forth. Finally he said, "You know nothing, you are barely seventy, you have learned nothing. I'm ninety-two, does that not tell you something?"

"It tells me that you're pretty proud of being ninety-two! And you haven't learned to respect work that isn't your own!"

"Excellent!" cried Wladyslaw. "You can be angry! Good, very good. But you haven't put any anger into your figures, and nothing else either. I'm telling you, they're mute! Well-drawn fairy-tale figures, fairy-tale idiots; look at their eyes, look at their hands, pathetic paws! Wait. I'll show you." He ran for his valise.

Among the socks, underwear, photographs, diverse belongings of all sorts, there were innumerable small packages, each wrapped in cotton wool held together with rubber bands.

"Look," he said. "My hands. You must learn while there is still time. Handling my faces could have taught you much, but these too can help you see that the simple line is utterly ignorant of the sculptural. Take away the cups, take everything off the table, clean it off. Your tea is far too weak."

Hand after hand was unpacked and laid before her, and she studied them in silence.

They were unbelievably beautiful. Shy hands, greedy hands, reluctant, pleading, forgiving, wrathful, tender hands. She lifted them, one after another.

It was already rather late at night. At last Mari said, "Yes, I understand." She paused briefly and went on. "Everything is here. Including pity. Wladyslaw, may I ask you a question? There on the train, on your long trip, didn't you feel at all sorry for all those hands and faces that you call raw material?"

"No," Wladyslaw said. "I no longer have time. I have already told you. I know them. I have forgotten my own face. I have already used it."

Mari went and turned off the tea water. "And?" she said.

"I must continue, filled only with my knowledge, my insight. But I have not yet been able to use the face of death, not well enough. He is too palpable. Or is it a she? In any case, a challenge that fascinates me. And what do you know of death? What do you think about it? Have you ever even experienced a great loss?"

"Wladyslaw," Mari said, "do you realize that it's three o'clock in the morning?"

"It doesn't matter. One must use the nights. My friend, I sense that you have not thought much about the face of death. And do you know why? Because you do not live with all your strength, all the time, in your own triumph dashing ahead of time, anticipating it and disdaining it. I am awake, always. Even in my brief dreams I continue to work, constantly. Nothing must be lost."

"Yes, Wladyslaw, yes," Mari said. She was very tired. From the depths of her exhaustion, where she no longer had the strength to follow what he was saying, she remarked that he had undoubtedly been very beautiful.

He answered gravely. "Very. I was so beautiful that people stopped on the street and turned around to look at me and I heard them say, 'It's not possible!'"

"That must have made you very happy."

"Yes. I liked it. I couldn't help it. But of course all of that took time from my work. I allowed feeling to dominate at the expense of observation. Much too often." Wladyslaw was silent for quite a while. Then he said, "Now perhaps we might have a meal to complete the day. You said something about beef?"

At four o'clock, the morning paper came through the letter slot.

"Are you tired?" Wladyslaw asked.

"Yes."

"Then I won't say much more. Just one thing – and now, my friend, you must give me your complete attention. It is simply this: do not tire, never lose interest, never grow indifferent – lose your invaluable curiosity and you let yourself die. It's as simple as that. No?"

Mari looked at him. She smiled without answering.

Wladyslaw took her hands in his. He said, "We have only two weeks. That will give us a poor fraction of all we have to talk about, all we must talk about. But do not be distressed; we will use the nights. Now you should sleep. Do not be surprised if I am gone when you wake up; I'll just be out for my morning walk. The city looks very provincial, but it does lie by the sea. When do the flower shops open?"

"Nine o'clock," said Mari. "And I've grown very fond of red."

Fireworks

"Is it your glasses?" said Jonna without looking up from her work. After a while she said, "Have you looked in all your pockets? The last place I saw them was in the bathroom."

Mari said nothing. Her steps went from the studio to the library and back again, to the bedroom, to the front hall.

"Tell me what you're looking for."

"Oh, some papers. A letter. It's not important."

Jonna stood up, went into the library, and looked under the table. There lay several sheets of blue paper covered with writing.

"She writes on both sides and doesn't number her pages," Mari explained. "Do you have time to talk?"

"No," said Jonna amiably.

Mari gathered up the papers.

"Okay, what does she want?" Jonna went on. "A brief summary."

"She wants to know what's the meaning of life," Mari said. "And she's in a hurry, she says."

Jonna sat down and waited.

"She thinks I have life experience, like you're supposed to have when you're old. What should I say?"

"Well, how old is she herself, this person?"

"She's not old – barely fifty."

"Poor Mari," said Jonna. "Say you don't know."

"I can't. And I can't say work is the most important thing because she doesn't like her job."

"What's her name?"

"Linnea."

"How about simply love?"

"Won't do! She's completely alone; no one loves her."

"And there's no one she cares about? No one to take care of?"

"Not that I know of."

"Does she read? Is she interested in world events?"

"I don't think so. Now you're going to ask if she has a hobby, but she doesn't. And she's not religious."

"This happens all the time," said Jonna. "Again and again. Now, once and for all, try to write down the meaning of life and then take a photocopy so you can use it again next time. I'm sorry, but I'm afraid you're going to have to deal with your Linnea by yourself."

"Oh, that's just wonderful!" Mari exclaimed. "Thank you very much. It's all very well and good for you. What do you care about the meaning of life? You don't have to explain it and don't get hard letters from people you've never met, and of course won't ever have to meet. And you've got someone else to compose your thank-you letters and sympathy notes and politely decline all the invitations you don't care for. Marvellous!"

Jonna stood with her back to Mari, looking out the window. "Of course. You're right. But come here a minute. The harbour is lovely in the fog."

The harbour really was lovely. Black channels cut through the ice all the way to the distant quays where the big ships lay barely visible.

"So terribly lonely," Mari said. "But Jonna, try to help me here. Could I write to her about experiencing very simple things..."

"Like what?"

"Well, for example, that spring is coming? Or just buying pretty fruit and arranging it in a bowl... Or a great, stately thunderstorm moving closer..."

"I don't believe your Linnea likes thunderstorms," Jonna said. And at that instant a skyrocket rose silently into the air far off across the harbour. The winter sky began to burst with repeated explosions of colour that paused for a few seconds in their beauty before sinking slowly and giving way to new multi-coloured roses, a lavish splendour repeated again and again, softened by the fog and for that reason more mysterious.

Jonna said, "I'll bet it's some foreign cruise ship entertaining its passengers. My, they're far away. Now a white one... That's really the prettiest because it makes the harbour look so black."

They waited, but nothing more happened.

"I think I'll go and work a little more," Jonna said. "Don't look so worried. Maybe your Linnea saw the same fireworks and it cheered her up."

"Not her! She looks out on a dismal courtyard, because her neighbour got the whole view of the harbour..."

"Neighbour?"

"Yes, a woman who just goes on and on about what she should do and what she should wear and what food she should buy and how to file her taxes and so on."

"Really?" said Jonna. "Remarkable. It seems to me there's a lot of affection in all that. I begin to suspect that maybe your poor Linnea did get a look at the fireworks after all and that she's getting along just fine. Write to her, now, and get it out of the way."

Mari sat down and wrote. When she was done, she went into the studio and asked if she could read it aloud.

"I'd rather you didn't," Jonna said. "Your juice is on the spice shelf. And take the torch, the light's out in the attic. Are you going to the post office tomorrow?"

"Yes. Do you want me to pick up your parcels?"

"I'll get them later; they're too heavy. But could you pick up some tomatoes and cheese and detergent on the way home? And mustard? I made a list. And put on something warm; they're saying it'll be down to ten degrees tomorrow. Now don't lose the list, and be careful on the street – it's going to be really icy."

"Yes, yes, yes," Mari said. "I know, I know."

On her way across the attic, Mari stopped as usual and gazed out across the harbour. She thought absent-mindedly of Linnea, who knew nothing about love.

Cemeteries

MARI DEVELOPED A SUDDEN INTEREST IN CEMETERIES the year that she and Jonna took their long trip. Wherever they went, she'd find out where the cemetery was and wouldn't rest until she'd seen it. Jonna was surprised, but resigned herself to this odd mania and supposed it would pass. It was wax museums the last time, but it hadn't lasted very long. She followed along obediently, up one street and down another through the grave keepers' quiet, neatly ordered villages, shooting a little film here and there, although she had never cared much for things that stood still. It was very hot.

"Of course it's very pretty," said Jonna experimentally. "But the cemeteries at home are much prettier, and you don't visit them."

"No," Mari said, "those are just people we know. These are more distant." And she changed the subject.

The graves Mari looked for were the forgotten, overgrown graves, and she stood by them for a long time, utterly content among the uncontrollable vegetation playing jungle across the hallowed ground. There was the same absolute feeling of calm on the Ile de Sein, the last sliver of land into the Atlantic, where the gravestones had sunk deep into the sand that continually drifted up and blew away again. They could just barely make out the texts that salt water and wind had tried to wipe away.

"And Pompeii?" Jonna suggested. "The whole city's a cemetery. Completely empty and anonymous."

"No," said Mari, "not empty at all. In Pompeii they're still there, everywhere."

They went to Corsica, to Porto Vecchio, and Jonna asked, "How about going on by bus? Then we wouldn't have to take a hotel for the night." She looked at Mari for a moment and added, "Well, whatever you want. We'll do the cemetery."

Here the stones carried photographs of the dead, stiffly staring photographs surrounded by wax flowers. In the hotel room, Mari tried to define it. "It was horrible... It makes them still there more than ever!"

Jonna was sitting at the table with the map and the bus schedule, making notes, considering, planning, and, when Mari repeated how horrible it was, she threw her notes across the room and burst out, "Horrible and horrible! Leave the dead alone and start behaving like you were alive! Be a travelling companion!"

"Forgive me," said Mari. "I don't know what's come over me." And Jonna said, "We'll give it some time. It'll be okay."

That evening, Jonna was filming in Porto, on a narrow street at the edge of town. All the windows and doors stood open because of the heat, and the light was red and golden in the sunset. Jonna filmed the children playing on the street, trying to get as much as she could until they suddenly realized what she was doing and went all unnatural, flocking around her and playing the clown.

"This won't be any good," she said. "Too bad. The light is so good."

When Jonna put the Konica in its case, a little boy came up to her with a drawing he'd made and asked if she'd film it for him.

"Of course," Jonna said, wanting to be nice. "I'll film you while you draw."

"No," said the boy. "Just the picture." And he held up his drawing. It was done with a thick felt pen on a piece of cardboard ripped from a packing box, perhaps, and the picture was very expressive.

"It's a grave," the boy said.

Very true, a distinct grave with a cross, wreaths, and people weeping. More interesting was the underlying cross-section of black earth and a coffin in which a person lay baring his teeth. An altogether gruesome picture. Jonna filmed it.

"Good," the boy said. "Now, for sure, he'll never come back up. I just wanted to make sure."

A woman came out on her steps and called to him. "Come inside," she said, "and stop this eternal nonsense!" She turned to Jonna and Mari and said, "You have to forgive Tommaso. He draws the same picture every time, and it happened a year ago."

"Was it his father?" Mari asked.

"No, no, it was his poor brother, his older brother."

"And they were very close?"

"Not at all," the woman answered. "Tommaso didn't like him, not a bit. I just don't understand the child."

She shoved the boy into the house. Before he disappeared, he turned and said, "Now, for sure, he'll never come back up!"

They walked back along the alley, the evening light still very red.

Mari repeated slowly, "Now, for sure, he'll never come back up..."

"I caught the red light," Jonna said. "And his eyes above the cardboard. It'll be good."

They travelled on to the next town and Jonna spread out the city map to find the cemetery.

"You don't need to look for it," Mari said. "I don't think I want to go."

"How come?" said Jonna.

Mari replied that she didn't really know; it just didn't seem important.

Jonna's Pupil

ONE AUTUMN, JONNA TOOK A PRIVATE PUPIL, a girl named Mirja. She was a large, unusually cheerless person who wore a cape and an artist's beret. Jonna declared that Mirja had talent, but that before anything could be done with it the girl would have to learn to respect her materials, which might take time. At the moment, she was leaving printing ink on the plates, digging deep holes in the jars of coloured ink, and tossing cotton waste in with the tarlatan – all unforgivable sins.

"I have to start right from the beginning," Jonna said. "She knows nothing of the serious facts of graphics; she just makes gifted pictures."

"How long is she going to be working with you?" Mari asked. "Are we going to feed her, too?"

"No, no, just coffee, maybe a sandwich or two. She's

always hungry. It makes me think of my own student days, when I never got to eat as much as I wanted."

On the days Mirja came, Jonna couldn't work with anything but Mirja. Mari kept out of the way and worried. Of course Jonna had a natural gift for teaching, she'd been an enthusiastic teacher at the Art Academy for many years, until she got tired of the whole thing and wanted to be left in peace with her own work. In any case, Mari thought, teaching, a real capacity to teach – that had stuck with her. She liked teaching. And Mari thought she understood the attraction of passing knowledge along in the hope that at least one person will manage to have a reasonable career... Nevertheless, Mari was highly suspicious of Mirja and her arty cape. Occasionally she'd ask how the instruction was coming along. Jonna answered curtly that at any rate her pupil had learned respect for the copper plates and had begun to clean up after herself.

"But you don't have to get meals for her, I hope."

"No, no, I told you. Just coffee."

Once, when Mari went over to Jonna's on the wrong day to borrow a pair of pliers, she walked right into a coffee break. There were two kinds of salad, Camembert, and small pasties. And the beef that Mari and Jonna were supposed to have the next day had been cut into elegant strips and decorated with parsley. On top of it all, Jonna had lit a candle on the table. They all had coffee. Demonstratively, Mari ate nothing. Mirja was extremely taciturn. After a while, she started drawing on her paper napkin with a charcoal pencil.

"What is that?" Mari asked.

"A sketch."

"Oh, yes, a sketch," Mari said. "That reminds me of art school. Everyone would go for coffee around the corner, and they'd sit and scratch something on their cigarette packs and say they'd had an inspiration. Well, well. How nice that some things don't change."

Jonna turned to Mirja. "You like the salad? Why don't you take it home?"

And the salad was packed in a plastic container, and, moreover, Mirja was given half the cheese and a jar of raspberry jam. When she'd gone, Mari said, "Doesn't she ever smile?"

"No. But she's making some progress. One has to be patient."

Mari said, "She's going to get fat if she goes on like that. Did you see what she put away?"

"Young people are hungry," said Jonna severely. "And I was just as shy when I was young."

"Ha!" said Mari. "She's not shy; she just won't bother trying to be pleasant. She thinks it's artistic to be gloomy. Can you show me any of her work?"

"No, not yet. She's finding her way."

Time passed, and Mari's irritation grew. The coffee threesomes had become a recurring, awkward phenomenon, but Mari couldn't keep from going over to see with her own eyes how shamelessly Jonna was spoiling her protégée. "Mirja, it's so cold out. Why don't you have a cap? I've told you you need a cap. Borrow mine." "Mirja, here's a list of the exhibits you should see."

"Here's the recipe for that salad. You could make it yourself." "Here are some books on graphic techniques; you ought to look at them..." It was incomprehensible that Jonna, who could be so chilly and distant, was now suddenly being a perfect wet nurse to a person who, in Mari's opinion, lacked every ounce of common civility, let alone charm.

Once, unforgivably, when Mari was alone in Jonna's studio, she turned over an aquatint that Mirja had done. It wasn't much good.

Autumn wore on. Jonna had set aside her own work and started building bookshelves that she didn't need. Mirja came regularly and was always equally hungry and dreary. One day Mari discovered that Jonna had begun giving Mirja vitamins, in a nice little bottle on the worktable.

"I see you're taking very good care of your daughter's health," Mari observed. "And you've put them in my bottle."

"Not at all – it's just a bottle like yours. You had yours this morning. Don't be childish."

And Mari went straight out, closed the door very slowly behind her, and stopped coming for coffee.

It was a sad time.

One evening in November, Mari came in and declared that now she wanted to see the worst movie Jonna could find: one with murders, preferably several. Jonna searched her video shelf. "Here's one that's pretty awful. I never dared show it to you."

"Good. Put it on."

When the movie was over, Mari drew a long breath. "Thank you," she said. "That feels better. Funny that Johnson would get all sentimental at the last minute; it wasn't his style at all. That homeless dog didn't fit."

"Of course it did. Johnson acts against his own true nature one single time, and you always have to pay for that. It was excellent bringing in an irrational detail. It would have been way too easy to have him simply bully his gang until they get rid of him."

"He couldn't help being the boss," Mari said. "He was a born leader. I suppose it went to his head. But they couldn't manage a single job without him telling them what to do... And what about afterwards?"

"No idea," Jonna said. "They just had to do it themselves. Anyway, it's only a B-movie. Maybe I'll erase the whole thing." She turned on the overhead light. "I was thinking of reading this evening. I don't feel like talking."

In the overhead light, the studio seemed oddly empty.

"Don't tell me you've cleaned?" Mari said.

"No. Don't you have anything to read? I've pulled out some books you might like. Short stories and stuff."

The studio really was very empty. And Mirja's smock was no longer hanging on its peg.

Mari opened one of the books. The evening was serene, no one called, the only sound was snowploughs rumbling along the street.

After a couple of hours, Jonna said, "I think I might take up lithography again. I mean, it's a possibility."

"Yes," Mari said. "A possibility."

"For that matter," Jonna went on, "did I ever tell you how when I was young I just marched out of their art school in the middle of the term so I could do my own work?"

"Yes, you did."

"Well, anyway, it was a real event in those days. A demonstration!"

"I know." Mari turned a page in her book. "That teacher you had, your professor? The one who was so overbearing?"

"Mari," said Jonna, "sometimes you're really a little too obvious."

"Do you think? But once in a while a person just needs to say what doesn't need to be said. Don't you think?"

And they went back to their reading.

Viktoria

THE ROOM HAD FOUR WINDOWS because the sea was equally beautiful in all directions. Now, as autumn approached, the island was visited by exotic birds on their way south, and it sometimes happened that they tried to fly right through the windows toward the daylight on the other side, the way they might fly between trees. The dead birds always lay with their wings spread wide. Jonna and Mari carried them down to the lee shore, where the landward breeze would carry them away.

Once Jonna said, "Now I understand what Albert meant when he said the lift of a hull is the same line you find in a bird's wing. When he was building *Viktoria*."

It had suddenly grown quite cold on the island. The wind had been rising all morning. *Viktoria* rode the swell inside the point, anchored on four lines. The way she always did in bad weather, of course, but they seemed to worry about her more every summer.

Jonna said, "I put new slip irons on her in May."

"You did. And checked her lines."

"Anyway, they said the wind would let up by evening."

But the wind didn't let up. Weather that keeps people from coming ashore or putting out to sea is good weather if you can pull your boat up on land. But they couldn't do that. *Viktoria* was now too heavy for them to pull out of the water. With the natural ease of a well-built boat, she danced on the waves that swept around the point toward her bow as well as on the breakers that washed straight through the lagoon toward her stern. But this was no time for admiration.

Mari said, "They were both called Viktor."

"What did you say?"

"That both our fathers were named Viktor."

Jonna wasn't listening. She said, "Go home and get warm until it's your turn to stand watch." And she stayed behind by the endangered boat and tried to think of a way of saving and preserving her. There had to be a way – maybe something very simple.

When it started to get dark, they traded places. Mari came down to the boat and Jonna sat down to draw new devices, possible new ways to bring *Viktoria* to safety in a storm. Trolleys and spars that couldn't be built. A winch, just as bad. A system of davits, no better. She made sketch after sketch and then threw them all in the stove. But she went right on trying to think up new unthinkable devices.

Darkness had fallen imperceptibly. Mari could make out almost nothing but the foam on the breakers. To the east, the seas broke over the rocks in a waterfall and crashed on through the lagoon. To the west, the breakers boiled around the point. There, somewhere in the middle, lay *Viktoria*.

After a while, Mari went back to the cabin.

"Well?" said Jonna.

"It's remarkable," Mari said. "Here in the house the storm sounds completely different. It sort of flows together; I mean like a long, humming tone. You tried to get it on a cassette once and it just sounded like an endless crunching..."

"How was she doing?" Jonna asked sharply.

"Good, I think. You can't see very much."

"You can use that acoustical stuff," Jonna said. "You seem to work a storm into almost everything you write. Did you check the stern lines?"

Mari said, "I think they're under water. It's risen."

They sat opposite each other at the table without talking. How Papa loved storms, Mari thought. The wind coming up would wipe away his melancholy and make him happy. He'd set the spritsail and take us out to sea...

Jonna said, "I know what you're thinking. That you always hoped for storms because they made him happy. And when a storm like this blew up, didn't he used to say 'I think I'll go down and look at the boat'? But you know, he just went out to look at the waves!"

"We knew that," Mari said. "But we didn't say anything."

Jonna went on. "It was certainly no trick for your father to pull up his boat; it was child's play. Shouldn't we eat something?"

"No," Mari said.

"Do you think there's any point in going down to have another look?"

"Hardly. There's nothing we can do."

"When was it we realized we couldn't do it any more? Years ago?"

"Maybe. It happened gradually."

"When you were dragging up stones from the anchorage."

"About then," Mari said. "But it was actually interesting, not being strong enough to lift and roll any more. It gave me ideas, you know – completely new ideas. About lifting, leverage, balance, angles of fall, about trying to use logic."

"Yes," said Jonna. "Trying to figure things out, I know. But don't talk to me about leverage right now. Is there anything left in that bottle?"

"A splash, I think." Mari went to get the rum and two glasses. The storm's humming monotone filled the room – steady, soporific, like an imperceptible trembling. They might have been on board a large steamer.

"He travelled a great deal," Jonna said.

"Well, yes, when he got grants."

Jonna said, "I'm not talking about your father. I'm talking about mine. He used to tell us about his trips. You never knew what he was making up and what really happened."

"Even better," Mari said.

"No, wait... They were awful, terrifying things, including storms, although he'd never been to sea."

"But that can make them even better," Mari said.

"You're interrupting. And when he was talked out and didn't know how to end it, he'd just say, 'And then it started to rain and everyone went home.'"

"Excellent," Mari said. "Wonderful. Endings can be really hard." She went to get the cheese and the crispbread and then went on. "He didn't tell us stories. He never talked much at all, now that I think about it."

Jonna cut the cheese in pieces and said, "We used to go to the library, the two of us. Just Papa and me. It was like being in his pocket."

"I know. He knew where the wild mushrooms grew, and he'd take us there and light his pipe and say, 'Family! Pick!' But he preferred going alone. Then he'd hide his mushroom baskets under a spruce and take us back with him at night, with torches, you know. It was frightening and wonderful. And he'd pretend he'd forgotten which spruce it was... And then we'd sit on the porch and clean mushrooms with the night all around and the kerosene lantern burning..."

"You said all that in some newspaper," Jonna said, and filled the glasses with the last of the rum. "Old Smuggler. Put that to soak; I want to save the label."

"Was he really brave enough to do serious smuggling?" Mari asked.

"Oh he was brave enough to do anything."

"But my father was social," Mari said. "You remember prohibition when Estonian vodka would float ashore and everyone went out to salvage it? Do you know what they did? They sold the canisters for huge sums of money! But he never did that. He let me go with him to search the beaches, young as I was. I'll never forget it. We hid the canisters in seaweed. He was adventurous."

"Wrong," said Jonna. "He was an adventurer. There's a big difference."

"You mean your father?"

"Of course, that's who I'm talking about. You know what I mean. He dug for gold, cut down enormous redwoods, built railways... You saw the gold watch he got in Nome when he was guarding fish, the one with the inscription?"

"Yes," Mari said. "A genuine Hamilton."

"Precisely. A genuine Hamilton."

It had now started to rain, and that wasn't good. A heavy rain could weigh down *Viktoria* and hamper her movements in the heavy seas. Mari tried to be funny. "And then it started to rain and everyone went home." But Jonna didn't laugh. After a while Mari asked, "Didn't he ever get homesick?"

"Yes. But when he came home he wanted to be off again."

"Mine, too," Mari said.

The rain got worse and worse – a real downpour.

Mari chattered on. "You know what he did when he got his government prize? He bought a paletot, you know – an overcoat. It was long and black and new, and he didn't like it. He said it made him feel like one of his own statues, so he went to Hesperia Park and hung it on a tree."

They listened to the rain.

"She'll get too heavy," Mari said. "And we can't get out to her to bail."

Jonna said, "Don't tell me things I already know."

They both knew well enough. The rain would go on, the boat would grow heavy, the waves would come in over the stern, she'd sink in her lines. But how deep would she sink, and would the rocks on the bottom knock her to pieces, or was it calm down there despite the storm, and how deep was it, how many metres…?

"Did you admire him?" Jonna asked.

"Naturally. But being a father wasn't easy for him."

"Not for mine, either," Jonna said. "It's funny. You actually know very little. We never asked, never tried to find out about the things that were really important. We didn't have time. What was it we were so busy with?"

Mari said, "Work probably. And falling in love – that takes an awful lot of time. But we still could have asked."

"Let's go to bed," Jonna said. "She'll probably make it. And anyway, it's too late to do anything about it."

The wind died toward morning. Freshly bathed and shiny, *Viktoria* lay at anchor as if nothing whatever had happened.

Stars

JONNA HAD A MATTER-OF-FACT RELATIONSHIP with Mari's brother Tom. They rarely saw each other in town, more often on the island, and then their discussions were practical. Tom would motor over to talk about lumber, special tools, maybe a generator that didn't want to work. It was barely three miles between their islands. Generally they got their machines running again, which gave Mari a secure feeling that most things here in life can be made to work.

She would stand for a long time and stare down his arrow-straight wake every time he drove back home. In June, Tom's island lay right in the sunset. Later the sun went down behind islands further south.

Once upon a time – astonishing but true – Tom and Mari had planned to emigrate to Tonga in the Pacific

Ocean. They displayed neither disappointment nor relief when Her Majesty's Service replied very politely that as a result of the recent typhoons they could not at the moment give any attention to immigration. Tom and Mari searched out a more northerly island and built a cottage and spent their summers there for many years. Tom wanted a skylight so he could look at the stars before he went to sleep, but the window leaked when it rained. Then they bought a telescope from an ad, unfortunately an older model that didn't make the stars very much bigger.

All of that was a very long time ago.

It was now already the end of August, and the sun was setting far south of Tom's island. There were no small boats on the water, only fishing boats, morning and evening, passing by with their black salmon flags fluttering at their sterns. But Tom was often out for the fun of it. Mari would see his boat heading straight out to sea, early and late.

"Jonna, listen to me. In those days we used to row, Tom and I. We rowed out to every skerry, the tiniest rocks, farther and farther out. Don't you ever want to go off to other islands?"

"But we're already on an island. They're all pretty much the same. And you can't go and waste a whole work day playing picnic."

One morning Tom came to get putty and window paint. He'd brought spring water and the mail. Mari had a letter from Johannes, one of the very few he'd ever written her.

"Jonna," she said, "Johannes wants to come and visit. You remember Johannes. Just for two days."

"But you know the cottage is too small. And the tent blew to pieces."

"I know, I know, but he doesn't want to stay in the cottage. He wants to sleep on an uninhabited island in a sleeping bag. He used to talk about it, but we never did it."

Tom thought of saying something but kept quiet.

Jonna said, "Don't you think Johannes is too old for a sleeping bag? And it's almost autumn. When is he coming?"

"Tomorrow," Tom said. "On the eleven o'clock bus from town. He called the store. I can go in and pick him up."

They thought about it.

"Have you got sleeping bags?" Tom said.

"Of course we have," Jonna said. She put the cans of putty and window paint in the basket and walked Tom down to his boat. They agreed that the best uninhabited island was Västerbådan, where it was easy to go ashore. The radio had promised clear weather.

Jonna said, "I'll pack some food for them."

"Good," Tom said. "As I recall, he doesn't think of stuff like that. So long."

"Bye."

That evening, Mari told Jonna things Jonna had long known but that now seemed important again.

"You know, Johannes and I had big plans and ideas, and one of the biggest was to live a natural life, peel away everything unnecessary, live in a cave or some such place – and try to grasp essentials. I know what you're going to say, but don't say it. Anyway, Johannes had his ideas long before the flower children came along!"

"This was in the fifties?"

"End of the forties, I think. But he never had time to live the natural life. And that time we collected money for that abandoned house in southern France and were going to invite friends who wrote or painted and needed a place to work in peace – but every time we'd got some money together, he'd give it to some strike fund... And the whole time we had this idea of living on an uninhabited island."

"Where do you sleep on an uninhabited island?" Jonna asked.

"Don't be dumb. I said sleeping bags."

"Did he believe all that stuff?"

"Of course! Naturally. But we never had the time."

"And now he's got the time?"

"No. No, I don't think so."

"I hope it goes well," Jonna said. "Anyway, I'm sending along sandwiches and coffee and some canned goods. Is there anything he specially likes?"

Mari answered immediately. "Baked beans. And he doesn't like coffee with powdered milk."

"Excellent, we're out of powdered milk. I'll go and look in the cellar."

Mari went out on the granite slope.

I know. I remember what he wants. To lie on his back in the heather and look at the stars a whole autumn night and listen to the sea without having to say a word. But there was never enough time... If only it doesn't get cloudy. Once he promised we'd live in a tent on Åland for a whole week, and I waited and waited but he sent word that he had too much editing to do... I borrowed a bicycle and pedalled all night. It was June and the nights were light and there were rosehips blooming everywhere and I found the village where his mother lived and she said, "Aha, so you're Johannes' friend. Come in and have some coffee." I could ride a bicycle again sometime; they say you don't forget, it's like swimming...

Mari and Jonna woke up early. The weather was clear and quite cold.

"So you don't want to take the primus stove?"

"No, no," Mari said. "It has to be a campfire. The campfire is very important."

Tom came right on schedule, a tiny dot in a straight line toward the island. Pretty soon they could see there was only one person in the boat. He jumped ashore and tied up. Johannes had called the store to say that he had too much work at the paper, unfortunately, and he was sorry.

"Oh, well," said Mari. "It doesn't matter." She turned abruptly and walked up toward the cottage.

Jonna was silent for quite a while.

Tom said, "Those old posts you were talking about. Shall we have a look?"

They went and looked at the posts. Some of them were only good for firewood, but quite a few could be used in Tom's new dock.

Jonna said, "It's funny about me, I've never really understood camping trips. Your sister gets a little too romantic at times. Changing the subject, are you busy with anything at the moment?"

"Just puttying the windows."

"Is it a long time since you slept in a sleeping bag?"

"Oh, maybe twenty years, I guess."

When Mari and Tom headed off for Västerbådan, Jonna stood watching until the boat disappeared behind the skerries. The wind had died.

That night she went out on the slope beside the cottage. Not one cloud disturbed the stars.

A perfect night.

The Letter

IT WAS NOT EASY TO SAY PRECISELY when the change had occurred, but Jonna was different. Very clearly, some-thing had happened. It wasn't something you noticed right away, not even enough to make you ask if she was feeling well or was upset about something. No, it was imperceptible, impossible to put your finger on. But it was there. No irritation, no depression, no pregnant silences, but Mari knew that Jonna was brooding about something she didn't want to talk about.

They saw one another only in the evenings, because Mari was making sketches for book illustrations, a big commission that made her both happy and anxious. When she came over to Jonna's, dinner was ready, they ate as usual with books beside their plates and watched television later. Everything was calm and exactly normal, but Jonna was somehow distant, far away somewhere. Mari had set the table with the wrong plates and forgotten the napkins, and Jonna said nothing. The man next door played scales on his piano and she didn't notice. Johnny Cash came on the radio and she didn't put in a cassette. It was frightening. When the film for the evening was over, she didn't say a word even though it was Renoir. They were sitting in the library, and to have something to do Mari started leafing through Jonna's mail, which lay in a pile of the table. Very quickly, Jonna reached for her letters and took them into her studio.

And then Mari dared say, "Jonna, is anything wrong?"

"How do you mean?"

"There's something wrong."

"Not at all. I'm working. I'm working well. I'm really getting into it."

"Yes, I know. You're not angry at me for some reason? No one's been mean to you?"

"No, no. I don't know what you're talking about." Jonna turned on the television and sat down to watch a stupid programme that was trying to be humorous, one of those programmes with an audience that laughs all the time.

Mari said, "Do you want some coffee?"

"No, thank you."

"Or a drink?"

"No. Make one for yourself if you want."

"Maybe I'll go home," said Mari and waited, but Jonna said nothing. So Mari made herself a drink, and, when she'd thought about it for a long time, she said as nicely as she could that Jonna meant so much to her that it would be completely impossible to get along without her.

But it was wrong, totally wrong. Jonna leaped up and turned off the television, and all her elusiveness and reticence vanished and she cried, "Don't say that! You don't know what you're saying to me! You're driving me to desperation. Leave me in peace!"

Mari was so astonished that she could only be embarrassed. They were both embarrassed. And then they both got very polite.

Mari said, "I think I'll do the dishes tomorrow, unless you're going to work very early."

"No, it'll be sometime after ten."

"I won't call, because I suppose you'll unplug the phone."

"Yes," Jonna said. "Do you have juice?"

"Yes, I've got juice. Good night."

"See you."

Mari didn't think she'd be able to sleep, but she fell asleep instantly before she even had time to realize how unhappy she was. It was only in the morning when she began to remember that she started feeling really, really bad. She had to repeat endlessly every word Jonna had said, the way she'd looked, the tone of her voice. And, mercilessly, how could she have said the things she'd said? Why, why, why? She wants to be rid of me.

Mari rushed across the attic and into Jonna's studio, and without the least consideration or diplomacy she cried, "Why do you want to be rid of me?"

Jonna stared at her for a moment. Then she said, "Read this," and handed her the letter.

"I don't have my glasses," said Mari angrily. "Read it to me!"

And Jonna read. She'd been awarded a studio in Paris for a year. The studio was meant for her use alone. The rent was very low. It was a great honour. Reply within ten days.

"Good Lord," said Mari. "Is that all!" She sat down and tried to rearrange her fears as best she could.

"So, you see, I don't know what to do," Jonna said. "Maybe the best thing would be to turn it down."

Any number of possibilities and impossibilities ran quickly through Mari's head – sharing the studio secretly; renting something nearby; coming to Paris later when her illustrations were done, which would only take a few months. She looked at Jonna and suddenly she understood. Jonna really wanted to work in peace, a whole year, now that she was working really well.

"The best thing is probably to turn it down," Jonna repeated.

Mari said, "Don't do that. I think it'll be all right."

"You do? You really think so?"

"Yes, I do. I'm going to need a long time for these illustrations. They have to be good."

"But I mean," said Jonna, quite confused, "illustrations..."

"Exactly. They have to be good, and that takes time. You may not realize how important they are for me."

"Of course I do!" Jonna burst out, and she launched into a long, earnest discussion of the importance of illustration, the painstaking labour, the concentration, the need to be undisturbed if you're going to do your best work.

Mari was hardly listening. A daring thought was taking shape in her mind. She began to anticipate a solitude of her own, peaceful and full of possibility. She felt something close to exhilaration, of a kind that people can permit themselves when they are blessed with love.